WHISPERING ALASKA

BRENDAN JONES

Delacorte Press

Text copyright © 2021 by Brendan Jones
Jacket art copyright © 2021 by Rowan Kingsbury
Interior illustrations copyright © 2021 by Rebecca Poulson

Visit us on the Web! rhcbooks.com

Educators and librarians, for a variety of teaching tools, visit us at RHTeachersLibrarians.com

Library of Congress Cataloging-in-Publication Data is available upon request.
ISBN 978-0-593-30353-5 (trade) — ISBN 978-0-593-30354-2 (lib. bdg.) — ISBN 978-0-593-30355-9 (ebook)

The text of this book is set in 11.75-point Bell MT Pro.
Interior design by Andrea Lau

Printed in the United States of America
10 9 8 7 6 5 4 3 2 1
First Edition

To Haley Marie, Kiera-Lee & Quinn.
You whisper the world to me.

In the deep glens where they lived all things were older than man and they hummed of mystery.

—Cormac McCarthy

The clearest way into the Universe is through a forest wilderness.

—John Muir

CONTENTS

PART ONE

From Pennsylvania to Alaska

CHAPTER ONE

Gulls cawed and dove outside Nicky's window as the RV rumbled down the steel ramp into the belly of the Alaska ferry. Nicky pressed her forehead to the smoked glass, the window splattered with mud and rain from three weeks of travel across the United States. A man wearing a protective mask waved them into the dim light. Her father checked his mirrors and slowed the vehicle as they bumped over the threshold.

Nicky unclicked her seat belt and scooted forward, resting her chin on her father's bony shoulder. "Hey, love," he said, brushing his whiskers against her cheek. "You ready for this?"

She peered out the windshield, watching the fluorescent lights move like clouds over the dashboard. Behind her, Josie took her iguana from her glass tank.

"I guess so."

"I can't believe Watermelon's going to Alaska," Josie mumbled.

"Iguanas love rainforests!" their father said, glancing in the mirror as he slowed to squeeze past a travel trailer that looked like a giant toaster oven.

"Uh—we're going to a *temperate* rainforest, with rocks, and ice, and trees. Iguanas come from *tropical* rainforests. Big difference, Dad."

A woman in low pigtails, also wearing a mask, made a fist as their father pulled into a spot. She flashed a thumbs-up, and he shoved the vehicle into park. The aluminum skin of the RV beside them reflected the mottled greens and browns of their camper.

"Girls," their father announced as the engine shuddered and went quiet. "I've been saving a joke this whole trip. You ready?"

Nicky smiled to herself as she walked back to retrieve her sunglasses. She was so tired of the ratty brown rug, the shards of oily potato chips that stabbed her bare feet, the musty scent of Watermelon's iguana poop drying under the heat lamp.

Their father did a drumroll with his fingers on the dashboard. "What do you call a fish with no eye?"

"We give up," Josie said quickly.

"*Fssshhhh,*" her father said. "Get it?"

"So, so dumb," Josie said, gasping. "Someone should report you."

Nicky flicked her eyes over Josie. Her twin had been crabby since Mount Rushmore.

"You can probably turn those off, Dad," Josie said as the windshield wipers moaned against the dry glass. "We're not moving, and it doesn't rain inside boats. Also, Nick, what's with the shades? It's not like you're a celebrity."

Their father switched off the wipers. Nicky slipped her sunglasses into her sweatshirt.

"Four more years before you drive, kiddo," her father said. "About the same amount of time it's going to take you to clean that green dye off your hands."

"Three. I get my learner's permit at fifteen," Josie shot back. "At least in Pennsylvania. And my hair color is called Evergreen."

As Josie swung open the door, a soda can rolled down the steps, clanking onto the concrete. Subway and McDonald's wrappers, along with a plastic Starbucks cup with whipped cream dried along the rim, littered the carpet. As the trio crossed the country, their father had favored drive-thrus and packaged food, obsessively cleaning each object with disinfectant wipes. If Nicky never took another bite of beef jerky, or saw another package of glazed sticky buns in her life, she'd be just fine.

Even though the first wave of the pandemic had passed, she understood her father's reluctance to fly. He chose their route according to which states were not shut down, tracking infection rates, and the number of positive cases as they considered where to sleep for the night. *Take no chances*, he told them. So they tolerated swabs stuck up their nose at least once a week. Covid-19 had already broken their family once. At the Presbyterian church, at their mother's funeral—it had all been a blur—he had vowed to both of them he would not let it happen again.

This meant they weren't even allowed to walk over to other sites at the RV parks. They couldn't use the bathrooms or playgrounds or pools or showers or splash parks—most were closed, anyway—or even go into the camp store without wearing an N-95 mask, no matter what the requirements were. "You're lucky I don't put you in a T100, with full facial protection," he told them.

Josie and Nicky knew better than to argue. They weren't about to pretend it couldn't touch them—it already had, and it continued to. Nicky would be looking out the window, watching buffalo charge into the hills of Yellowstone National Park, and there her mother would be. Standing at the top of a hill. Watching her.

As they started to unload their bags from the RV, Josie tapped Nicky's shoulder and whispered, "Hey. Do you think Mom ever would have *dreamed* of sleeping on a boat?"

"Maybe," Nicky said. "She liked adventures."

"Trips to the Jersey Shore. Not across the whole country. To Alaska. On a *boat*," Josie huffed.

Their parents had met at an open-mic night in Danville. Her mother had heard her father play guitar, and—as she told it—couldn't think straight afterward. She called him for lessons. The rest, her father liked to say, winking at the twins, was history. Their mother always shushed him when he said, "If it weren't for guitars, you two wouldn't be alive."

A couple of times, Nicky had caught them, in the kitchen or in their bedroom, singing together. *If a tinker was my trade, would I still find you?* Then her mother's deep alto voice would chime in. *I'd be carrying the pots you made, following behind you.*

This line always made Josie laugh, because both she and Nicky knew that their mother led their family, even if their father had worked hard giving lessons and tending bar to put their mother through medical school. "You girls wouldn't be living in a beautiful old house like this, or riding in a shiny black pickup, if it weren't for your dad."

As Josie shuffled through her backpack, Nicky searched for the right response, finally giving up. "I guess I don't really know," she admitted.

Josie snorted. "*I* do."

Aside from a couple trips to Philadelphia, or the New Jersey Shore to see their grandparents, their family hadn't really left Danville much. Josie's mother was always working in the hospital emergency room, which she vowed one day to direct. They went to Knoebels, the amusement park across Interstate 80 that had the Phoenix, the wooden roller coaster her mother loved to ride. Or hiking in Ricketts Glen. That was about all.

Josie slipped the hood of her Danville Ironmen sweatshirt over her head. "Now that I think about it, Mom didn't like adventures at all. She liked work, and her yoga, and coming home in the evenings. In fact, she would have thought we were being cowards, running away from home like this. Leaving the house, and our lives, behind."

Nicky didn't know if she agreed with this. Nevertheless, she kept her mouth shut, focusing on packing for the next three days on the ferry.

7

Even though they were technically called "mirror twins," Nicky found that her thoughts rarely matched her sister's. As Josie always said, if you put two mirrors together, you just got infinity. No end, no beginning. They were reflections of each other, their mother had told them. "When you're unsure about something, just look at your sister, and you'll see things more clearly. Never forget, you girls are so lucky to have one another."

Though they both had dimples and strawberry-blond curls—at least when Josie didn't dye hers Christmas-tree green—Josie's parted to the left, and Nicky's to the right. Josie wrote with her right hand. Nicky wrote with her left. The birthmark they had each been given by their mother, the one she always said resembled an upside-down Sicily, appeared on opposite shoulder blades. Even their organs were on opposite sides—including their hearts. Josie's was on the left—the "normal" spot for a heart, as she never tired of pointing out—while Nicky's lived on the right side of her chest. Which meant that when they hugged, they could feel the other's heart beating just inches from their own.

Since leaving Danville, Nicky couldn't once recall hugging her sister.

Nicky had overheard her mother tell her father that she thought the girls used different sides of their brains to understand the world. "Nicky drops into her own universe," her mother had said. "She's probably more like you in that way. She's the storyteller. The right-brained one."

Nicky often wondered what her mother had meant by this. Her mother understood everything about the body, so she wouldn't have made the comment without knowing exactly what she was talking about.

It made sense to her that if their hearts were on opposite sides of their bodies, then they'd also be controlled by opposite hemispheres of the brain. It was also true that Nicky liked art, drawing with colored pencils, and cutting out collages. She preferred a walk in the fields or fishing in Uncle Max's pond to writing English papers or solving math problems—that was Josie's realm. Nicky liked working for Uncle Max, tallying her hours helping him stack bales of hay in the barn, sweeping out the corncrib, raking leaves from beneath the black walnut and setting the piles on fire.

But what about the other part, about being able to drop into her own world?

In the four months since her mother had died, she'd found herself aching to ask her mother what she had meant. Nicky knew her mother didn't approve of hiding from anything, so she wanted to confront this truth. She often told the girls to "trust in what is difficult," because difficult things made you stronger. Once, she had caught Nicky reading a fantasy book. "You need to learn to cope in a world without elves and unicorns," she said, taking the book away. Nicky never saw it again.

All Nicky knew for sure was that when she climbed to the top of Uncle Max's farm, passing beneath the big Chinese chestnuts, her world evened out. She had never mentioned this to either of her parents, or even to her sister—how, in the shadows of trees, where the beeches grew among the furnaces and farm machinery rusting back into the soil,

Nicky could sometimes hear the tiniest whisper of the beech saplings as they pressed up through the leaves, and even feel a current, or even a tremor in the ground when she removed her rubber boots. It wasn't the Phoenix at Knoebels, or the baseball games by the Susquehanna River, or even her room or her friendships that thrilled her. It was walking beneath the trees in World's End State Forest, or Ricketts Glen, or Uncle Max's farm. Listening to the crisp shirring of the leaves in the fall, which almost sounded like breathing.

"Hey," her sister said as she zipped up her backpack. "Paging Nicole Hall from whatever universe she's traveling through. Please reconnect with your terrestrial body so we can complete this bizzarro journey and resume something approaching a normal life. Are you packed?"

"I'm here," Nicky said, zipping her bag.

"Everyone have what they want?" their father asked. "Three nights on this old scow. Better get warm clothes."

"I can't wait for a real bed," Josie said, sighing.

Their father's army duffel thudded onto the concrete. Then he crouched and pulled both girls into his arms. His whiskers felt scratchy against Nicky's cheek. He smelled like sweat and pistachios, which he had eaten the whole way across the country, flinging the shells out the window, despite Josie's accusations of littering.

"Girls," he said as he held them. "Do you know how much I love you?"

"Dad, can we not do this right now?" Josie said, rolling her eyes and squirming to get away.

He cleared green curls from Josie's cheeks. Nicky could

see from his pink eyes and flushed cheeks that he was crying. "I want you to know that you are two of the strongest, most impressive kiddos I've ever seen. When we drive off this boat, we'll be in Alaska. Can you believe that? Aunt Mall and your cousin Clete, who's just your age, will be waiting. Maybe Uncle Cliff will take us on his boat to fish for salmon. Or we'll go looking for grizzly bears. But the most important thing is that we're a family. Together."

"What about you?" Josie asked, breaking from his grasp. "What are you going to do on this island? Are you going to find a job?"

His smile vanished. "Aunt Mall works for the newspaper, and she's asking around. But don't worry about me." He pointed his fingers at them, finding his smile again. "We're the Halls, right? We always find a way from one room to another."

"Dad," Josie groaned. "Of all your dumb sayings, that's the one I hate most."

Josie pulled her curls back into a high ponytail. She clicked her yoga mat onto her backpack, folded her fleece pants and set them into the top compartment, followed by slippers and her collared purple soccer shirt. She rapped her knuckles on her camping mug. "Let's go find our cabin."

Her father lifted his guitar case out of the camper, then shoved a raincoat, a pair of Levi's, his toiletry kit, and his old, scratched steel mug into his duffel. He pulled the brim of his Danville Ironmen baseball cap, which showed a single muscled arm holding a thick hammer, low over his eyes. Then he held up a tent bag with the tags still attached.

"What's that? Oh no," Josie said. "No way."

Their father slung his duffel over a shoulder. "Yes way. We sleep outside. Just like I did when I was young like you. The sun and salt are bad for the virus. Masks up, girls. Forward march. We're moving out." He started toward the stairs.

"I'm *not* sleeping outside!" Josie shouted, the last of the words muffled as she pulled her mask over her nose. She pulled it down again. "That's just a theory that it's safer."

"No one *knows* anything," their father said, holding open a steel door. Nicky heard an edge in his voice as she passed him to start climbing the stairs.

"Hey! What about those signs on the wall?" Josie yelled. "At least can we use the elevator."

"Alaskans don't use elevators," their father shouted back. "Plus, it's not safe. C'mon. Or I'll start telling another joke."

Josie's flip-flops clapped against the concrete as she pushed past Nicky, charging up the stairs. Her bag shifted from side to side like a loose turtle shell. Her words echoed in the stairwell. "I—hate—this SO MUCH."

Nicky kept her pace, watching as the stairs passed beneath her. She stopped when she didn't hear her father behind her. Then she turned, holding the railing so the weight of her bag wouldn't send her toppling. He gazed into the parking lot, his red glasses hanging around his neck, holding the door open. As if waiting for one last person.

Then he shook his rust-red hair and started up the stairs. The door slammed shut behind him.

CHAPTER TWO

E ight flights of stairs later, Nicky caught up with Josie, who was leaning against the wall, trying to catch her breath. Without a word Nicky passed her sister and pushed the door at the top, which groaned as it opened, letting in a gust of moist salt air. She put a hand up to fend off the glare as the sun poked out of the clouds, making the deck and railings shine.

Half of the deck was protected from the weather by a glass ceiling. On the other half, toward the back of the boat, Nicky counted eight, nine, ten tents, each set up inside squares marked out with black tape, the quadrants spaced six feet apart. "We've got a mandolin player," their father said, coming up behind them and nodding toward a corner where a white-haired man wearing oil-stained jeans and a tattered yellow rain hat plucked away.

"Talk about unsafe!" Josie said, pulling off her mask. "We might as well be in the city. Riots, sickness. Everyone squished together. There's no way we're sleeping in a tent out here."

Their father scanned the deck, shading his eyes against the sun. "Look! The rain has cleared. People are distancing. The deck is taped off. It's just like the old homesteaders, each with our own plot of land. C'mon, pioneers!"

The squelch of duct tape and sounds of harmonica and mandolin filled the air as they walked toward an open spot in the corner, near a young couple lashing down a red tent. The man wore a newborn on his chest. "Shall we put down our stake here, girls?" their father said, dropping the tent onto the concrete.

The young couple nodded a greeting. Josie gestured at the horizon, where gray clouds gathered. "We're going to wake up underwater."

Their dad laughed. "That's east, J. The weather's behind us. Only sunshine from here on out. A thousand miles north, and we're home."

Josie lifted her eyebrows at Nicky, questioning their father's idea that "home" existed on an island of the Alaskan panhandle. Or that the sun always shined in the rainforest.

Nicky let it pass. She didn't much care anymore. After almost a month in the camper, with the taupe furry ceiling just above her head, she wanted to wake up in a place where she could think of her mother coming home from the hospital, turning the shiny black pickup in to the driveway, waving at them through the windshield. Telling them that she was fine, and that everything would soon return to normal again.

When she got no response from Nicky, Josie turned and

said, loud enough for people around them to hear, "Mom would have *hated* this."

Their father froze. Slowly, he picked up the tent from the deck and set it down on a white plastic beach chair. He zipped his black windbreaker to his Adam's apple and squinted at the sun setting over the water.

"Maybe," he said. "Maybe she would have. But she's not here anymore."

"That doesn't mean we're not allowed to think of her feelings," Josie said, her voice trembling. "And that doesn't mean we can't count the days until we're allowed to make our own decisions. Five years and 323 days"—she glanced at her watch—"nine hours and thirteen minutes."

"You can think of her feelings," their father said. "Think of what she would say, and do—think of all of it. But right now, what's important is that we're here, together. On the way to an island in Alaska where your aunt, uncle, and cousin are waiting for us."

Josie's face remained scrunched up while her father just stood there looking over the water.

Even if it had been the wrong thing to say, Nicky knew her mother would have hated the ferry. Sleeping in a tent, making food in a cafeteria. The smell of ammonia from the seagull poop. No place to run, or private area where she could do her yoga. Her mom coughed easily, because her lungs were weak. She walked her bike up the hills around Danville that the the twins could easily climb. She was always joking that her lungs would do her in, while at the same time exercising to make them stronger.

The virus took a family joke and turned it serious. Both of Estelle Parisi Hall's daughters had grown up accustomed to seeing her in a long white coat, chestnut hair tied up in a bun, hazel eyes unblinking as she bent over a clipboard, explaining to patients in the emergency room what she had done, or what she could do, to make them better. It still seemed like some awful dream, watching through the glass at the ICU—her mother had convinced the hospital to let her family in—seeing her mother's tan, healthy skin pale and her hair turn wiry and gray.

Nicky hated her sister for bringing their mother up like this. How her mother had asked one of the nurses to dye her hair back to brown while she was in her bed. The job wasn't perfect, but she looked more like herself. Nicky cringed with the memory. She just wanted a calm place where she could allow herself to recall her mother when she was healthy— her spiced scent, and the feel of her hands, warm from doing the dishes at night, rubbing the back of Nicky's neck.

For a couple weeks after their mother's death, Nicky was convinced Estelle would simply appear. In the shade of Uncle Max's corncrib, or at the crest of his farm, looking out over the Susquehanna Valley. Or even with a fishing rod at the pond, standing in Uncle Max's grove of Norway spruce, or knee-deep in the spring corn. Nicky listened for the shuffle of her mother's espadrilles in the dirt, the low murmur of her voice as she explained how the valley had once been underwater. How the corn furrows were once home to trilobites and periwinkles, their shells now inscribed into stones that farmers tossed off to the side so their tractors wouldn't flip.

Tent poles clattered about as Josie dumped the contents of the tent bag onto the concrete deck. Nicky stared at the mess of red fabric. This was what Josie did when she went too far. Create a problem, then solve it.

"I don't even care where I sleep. I just want to be in one place," Josie announced by way of truce.

"Me too," Nicky said quickly, eager to bring things back to normal. Anything to make these last three days of their trip to Jackson Cove, Alaska, peaceful. She just wanted to get to the ferry terminal on Friday, where Aunt Mall and her cousin Clete waited, like presents to be unwrapped.

"Great," their father said, smiling back at them. "Let's get this tent built."

Nicky picked up the instructions. Josie grabbed Nicky's aviator glasses from her sweatshirt pocket and put them on, peering over her shoulder. Nicky glimpsed her own reflection in the lenses, her strawberry-blond curls blowing across her eyes as she unfolded the directions in the sunlight.

"Are you looking at yourself? Don't be weird." Josie said, snatching the paper from her hands. "Okay. Nick, put all the poles together, and lay them out there. Insert the tip of the pole A into C. This shouldn't be difficult."

The sun slipped behind a cloud. Nicky fit the poles together, watching her sister out of the corner of her eye as she read.

Since kindergarten, Josie and Nicky had been in the

same class. Book reports, science fairs, sports teams—Josie breezed through all of it, approaching each task with the same dogged, methodical attitude. Lanky and purposeful, she memorized speeches, aced math tests, and never seemed to care what others thought of her. When she brought in the iguana for Show Your Pet Day, Nicky's friend Sonya made a joke about Watermelon's name. Josie delivered back such a sharp response that she had people laughing and scared at the same time. "What's that goblin you brought? I thought Snickerdoodles were cookies, not dogs."

Even with her more recent moves—dyeing her hair, becoming a vegetarian, and her infatuation with yoga—Nicky was pretty sure that as soon as her sister arrived in Jackson Cove, she'd have people copying her. Suddenly the pharmacy on the island would be out of green hair dye—if it even carried hair dye in the first place. Like her mother had always observed, Josie marched to the beat of her own drum.

Though every once in a while, she relaxed her guard, and then the two sisters would charge around with their mother through the grass fields behind Uncle Max's farmhouse, catching fireflies in mason jars. Josie kneeling as her mother made surgical holes in the lids with her pocketknife, dropping in blades of grass as Uncle Max drank a mint julep. Nicky watching as her sister lifted the jar to eye level to peer inside, the collective glow of the fireflies lighting up Josie's light freckles and rare smile.

The tent started to rise, the pole making a neat arch. "Yeah!" their father said, coming back to life as he watched them. He slapped his baseball cap against the railing. "Look at that. My two girls. Building us a home."

A horn sounded from above. Nicky and Josie ran to the railing to watch the workers below retrieve the thick ropes connecting the ferry to the dock. The boat started to drift. A second horn blew, and Nicky's rib cage rattled as they powered forward. Gulls came together and tore apart, shrieking just above their heads.

"Kiss the rest of the United States goodbye," their father said from behind them. He squeezed Nicky's shoulder. She could feel his excitement through his fingers. "You guys are each going to have your own bed up in the attic of this miner's house Aunt Mall found us. It's just up the hill from the harbor in town."

"Your Alaska dream," Josie muttered. "Just what I've always wanted."

He went on, ignoring Josie. "You're going to learn all about how the Russians came to the island and fought the Tlingits for the land. Land that your uncle's family has lived on for ten thousand years. Can you imagine that? Ten thousand years."

Nicky watched as the brick ferry terminal grew small behind them. An American flag snapped in the wind above a larger midnight blue flag showing the stars of the Big Dipper, and the North Star. She watched the rush of water beneath her, trying to imagine the world below, but seeing nothing.

"I need coffee," their father announced, suddenly sounding tired.

He left them, slipping his mask back over his ears. Nicky dropped her head against her sister's shoulder, which felt hard against her temple. Their mother had given them both olive skin, narrow noses, and large, wide-spaced hazel eyes. They got their dimples and their lighter, slightly reddish curls from their father. Uncle Max called them "Ellis Island Twins," because of their mixed heritage, or just "The Mutts," though their mother always scolded her younger brother. "Don't tease my girls," she'd say, pulling them close.

Nicky rose to wrap her arms around Josie and tell her how much she loved her, and to feel her heart against her own. But Josie seemed to anticipate the move, and she pulled back.

"You know we're on our own now, right?"

Nicky blinked. The lowering sun lit up her sister's faint freckles. Her green-brown eyes focused on Nicky, unwavering.

"What do you mean?"

"I mean we're twelve. No one on this island's going to tell us what to do."

Nicky felt her heart cool. "I guess. How is it any different than Danville?"

Josie stared back over the water. "You're a young twelve, Nicky. Just like Dad. Only difference is he's forty-one. Me, I'm more like Mom."

Nicky didn't know what to say to this. She only knew that her sister's words hurt.

Josie shook her head and started off for the stairs. "Just like I thought. You wouldn't understand."

20

Nicky blinked back tears as her sister took off, grinding her molars as the churn of water behind them blurred. Just because Josie and her mother could both solve math problems, or put together puzzles, didn't mean that Josie was more like their mother.

When the virus first broke out, Nicky had overheard a conversation between her parents in her father's woodshop.

"There's no reason for you to go to the hospital," her father hissed. "You have an underlying condition."

"That's not how I work," her mother responded. "You know that."

"You're putting yourself in danger, with your lungs. You're putting *us* in danger."

"I'm a medical doctor," her mother had said. "This is what I *do*. It's what supports us, and it's how I feel useful. This was our plan, and I'm not going to let some virus stop us. I took an oath. The whole point of being an ER doctor is to be there in a crisis. *This* is a crisis."

Nicky's breath went shallow. She tried to swallow back the sadness of knowing the person she loved most on this earth had known what she was doing, living in a separate wing of the house, waving to them in the morning from out the window before climbing into her pickup to go to the hospital. An essential worker—no one more essential than her mother. She stopped using their kitchen, which meant the stove got crusty from her father's fry grease, and the refrigerator emptied out until it was just milk and eggs, the trays sticky from where the sugar-free syrup he let them dump on their toaster waffles dripped. Had their mother really thought she was keeping them safe, when she took the risk of continuing to work in the most dangerous place in the hospital, the ER? The question felt like a stone lodged in Nicky's throat.

Nicky just wanted this travel, this movement, to be over. No more Uno, no more breaking down the dinette table to make Josie's bed in the RV, no more sleeping in Walmart lots, masking up and wandering the aisles for breakfast when the stores opened, before the crowds arrived. No more waking to the rumble of the engine as her father pulled onto the interstate and reached forward to reset his mileage counter for the day.

She did like the RV parks—the whoosh of the air conditioner as their father locked in the fifty-amp cord and attached the drain so they could shower and do dishes without worrying about water. Nicky would light citronella candles as their father unzipped his guitar case. Josie unrolled her mat by the firepit to do yoga while Watermelon perched on a nearby rock. Nicky would watch from her camp chair as the candle guttered, the sparks rising from the fire, pulsing for a moment before rising into the dark.

People often gathered near their campsite, careful to keep their distance, remaining just outside the circle cast by the flames as they listened to her father play his guitar. As she sat in the glow of the fire, Nicky would close her eyes, watching the music rise against the backs of her eyelids. Letting her mind wander down a path that led to a truth she knew she needed to hear, but didn't yet have the courage to listen to.

Their father had promised that this journey would change them, lighten their spirits, and get them grounded. What he didn't understand, Nicky thought, was that their lives had already changed. The anger over having a mother, and then, in the space of just a few weeks, not having a mother, had spun them around until they didn't know which way was up. The trip had also changed her relationship with her sister. Their father seemed too caught up in his own sadness to see that.

"You okay, sailor?"

The older man who had been playing mandolin observed her from beneath his yellow rain hat. He had a lined face, and pale blue eyes rimmed with red.

She nodded.

The man opened his arms, and Nicky saw two golden eyes peering back at her. "This here's Rooster, my cat. She can't stand to be alone, which is why I brought her up from the truck."

The cat blinked at her, then burrowed farther into the man's coat. Nicky gave a polite smile, laughing in her head at a female cat named Rooster. She let the wind push her hair from her face, then focused on the crumpled water far below.

When she looked back again, both man and cat were gone. She couldn't see the ferry terminal behind her, just ribbons of whitewater in their wake as the boat sailed north, picking their direction for them.

CHAPTER THREE

"Hey," her father said that evening as he and Nicky crouched in the tent. "Hey, Nick."

"Yeah?"

They sat in a nest of sleeping bags, spooning soup from mugs they had heated in the cafeteria. Josie stayed outside, holding her phone above her head to capture the last bit of signal in the United States so she could post a photo on Instagram before they crossed the border into Canada.

Her father stared up at the tent ceiling. "Okay, get ready. Why did Humpty Dumpty have a great fall?"

"I have no idea," Nicky said, crumbling crackers into her soup. "He lost his balance."

"To make up for his terrible summer! That one's perfect for us, right?"

Nicky nodded.

Though it was past nine, the tent fabric still glowed with the last light of day. She could hear the flap of the flags just outside, and the rush of ocean as the ferry pushed through the waves.

"The book Aunt Mall sent me says there are four main kinds of trees on the island. Sitka spruce, western hemlock, yellow cedar, and red alder," Nicky said.

"There are going to be more trees than you can imagine," he said, tipping his cup back to drink the hot soup. "Even more than Oregon or Washington. You'll love it."

"Most of it is hemlock," Nicky said. "No beeches, or oaks, or black walnuts. That's okay, though."

"Did Josie's friend Veronica tell you that?"

Somewhere around the middle of the country, Josie had started communicating with a seventh-grader in Jackson Cove who ran the Drama, Debate, & Forensics team. Veronica had asked Josie to prepare a tryout speech so she could make it onto the team before school started.

"No. I haven't met her."

"Did Josie choose a subject for her speech? Maybe Teddy Roosevelt?"

Nicky shook her head. "I doubt it. She hates him."

Josie had insisted on making a detour to Mount Rushmore, saying that she wanted to check on whether a team of mountain climbers had done a good job sealing cracks on Theodore Roosevelt's chin. At first her father said that South Dakota was out of the way, and the park would be too crowded. But he finally gave in. Despite Roosevelt being fifty-five feet tall with a perfect chin, Josie declared him a disappointment, a racist who enjoyed killing Indigenous

Americans, and didn't believe Black people should have the right to vote. He probably was just as bad as the Russians in Sitka, Josie had observed. Same story: sail onto the island and kill everyone in sight.

A similar thing happened when they went to Yellowstone. It was a place Josie had been aching to see since she was little, when their mother had told them stories of explorers in the 1800s who tried to use the Old Faithful geyser to wash their clothes. Their wool sweaters and pants had been ripped to shreds.

But when they got there, Josie complained that the semicircle viewing station disrupted the proper flow of water from the eruption. The crowds were stupid, with too many people holding their phones up for video. Some of them weren't wearing masks, and no one had any consciousness of social distancing. Nicky didn't tell her she agreed.

When they reached the high desert of eastern Washington, Josie had started to cry in great heaves. Just outside Spokane, she insisted on stopping at a pharmacy. She pulled on her mask and disappeared inside. That night she emerged from the camp shower with deep green curls. Their father said nothing, even when the RV park attendant pointed to the spot in the contract where it said visitors couldn't use sinks to dye their hair. He paid a hundred dollars in damages, and they pushed on toward the coast.

Soon after that, in the aisles of the supermarket above the Alaska ferry terminal in Bellingham, Washington, Josie announced that she was becoming a vegetarian. Also, her long-held plan of going to Deep Springs, a college in

California's desert where could learn Greek and take care of cattle—started for boys, but her mother told her that didn't matter—was no more. She declared that when she turned eighteen, she planned to go to India, to meditate and do yoga, and perhaps follow a guru. Neither Nicky nor her father said a word.

The tent entrance unzipped, and Josie burst in, slipping off her sneakers and flashing her headlamp around. "I posted the sunset. I'll bet it's going to break like a hundred likes. That sunset's going to get like one point two thousand likes. And check this out." Josie crouched between them and held her phone up. "Veronica is so cool."

A girl with high, polished cheekbones and a gentle smile appeared. She wore a thick wool turtleneck sweater and jeans with the cuffs rolled. She stood on a rocky beach, the ocean lapping against the stones behind her.

"Hi, Hall family!" she began. "My name is Veronica, and I wanted to make a short video to welcome you onto our island. As you probably know, your daughter is *awesome*, and it's so cool she reached out before you guys got here. She's told me about you two, and Nicky, you'll love all the forest we have around us—it's crazy, you can't look anywhere without seeing a tree. Mr. Hall, I know your sister, Mallory—meaning, I read her articles every morning. I think you're going to love life on the Rock, as we call it; I know that makes it sound like a prison colony or something, but it's not! Oh, and I just wanted to say I'm so excited to have Josie as part of our Drama, Debate, & Forensics team. Her speech is going to be awesome. I wish you all weren't coming at the end of the summer, because everything smells like dead fish, and the storms start, and it gets dark. But you'll love it anyway! Safe journeys on the Alaska Marine Highway—that's what we call the ferry—and can't wait to meet all of you for real. Bye!" She waved vigorously at the camera, giving a wide smile that seemed to light up their small tent.

"Isn't she the best?" Josie asked, looking at them.

Their father reached out to ruffle Josie's hair. "I'm so proud of you, connecting like this even before we've arrived."

"It was only because they want the tryout video for the DDF team. Then we started talking, and we were insta-friends," Josie said as she got situated in her sleeping bag. "Veronica told me she memorizes all her debate team speeches, just like I do. She's never gotten a question wrong on her math tests. She sits in the back of the class and day-dreams, and only speaks to correct the teacher. I think we're going to be best friends."

"It's great she reads Aunt Mall's articles," their father said. "Nicky, maybe you guys can be friends too."

Nicky watched as Josie patted around, searching for her soup. "Veronica's family lived in Seattle before coming to Alaska. Her dad sold his start-up, and they decided to move out of the city. Her mother's Tsimshian Indian, and her dad's Black. The Tsimshian used to be enslaved by the Tlingit, and the other way around, but Veronica says the tribes get along now and everyone just accepts that the land is really Tlingit land," Josie said, addressing Nicky.

"Great!" their father said, after a pause. "So proud of you."

"You already said that. She also showed me her boots, which she says everyone on the island wears. Big brown boots to keep out the mud and rain. Her family is devoted full-time to keeping Alaska wild. I think she's the smartest person I've ever talked to. I actually can't wait to meet her for real. Her videos are so funny. Where's my soup?"

"Right there by your sleeping bag," their father said. "Don't shine that light in my eyes."

"Oh, and I checked out the Facebook group her dad monitors. It's called Jackson Cove Convos. She had already heard we were coming to the island. Word is out. All anyone is commenting about is Covid-19 regulations, and when they're going to cut down the forest behind town. Veronica's *totally* against it. She's doing a speech on Wednesday, a week from now, at the town hall."

"Josie," her father grumbled, shielding his eyes. "Please watch where you shine that thing."

She reached up to her head to switch off the lamp. "This tryout speech for Drama, Debate, & Forensics is a formality, Veronica said. She's more worried about speaking at town hall. Can you believe anyone clearcuts? I thought that was only in the olden days. We'll be living in a wilderness that is seventeen *million* acres. Nine point six million acres of trees, definitely enough for you to get lost in," Josie said to Nicky. Her tone suggested that Josie wouldn't mind if Nicky did just that. "The rest is rock and ice. It makes Uncle Max's farm, or even the Alleghenies, feel so small."

"Or Yellowstone," Nicky added.

"Yellowstone's an amusement park," Josie scoffed. "With a very big fountain. I hate it."

"Good thing we have Aunt Mall, Uncle Cliff, and Clete to show us around our new home," their father said.

"Would you stop saying that?" Josie snapped, picking up her soup. "There are more folks at the county fair in Danville than in all of Jackson Cove. Not only are we going to an island with no virus, we're going to an island with no *people*. Surrounded by *nothing*!" Josie exclaimed. "Which is great, because it means people will just let nature be."

"As long as we don't bring the virus, I guess it's okay," their father said, in a softer voice.

"Yeah, so long as we don't catch it on this boat. Veronica said there are as many grizzly bears as there are humans on the Rock," Josie said. "Can you believe that? About two thousand. I wouldn't feel so bad if a grizzly bear ate me. Even better, a polar bear, since they'll all be extinct in the next fifty years. Think about that. The Arctic paved over with shopping malls with penguin petting zoos. In fact, feeding a polar bear with my body would be an honor."

Their father let out a snort. "Let's see if you say that when a bear's chomping your arm off."

The ferry rumbled beneath them. Josie unzipped her sleeping bag and shoved her legs inside and glared at him. "As soon as this virus is over, Veronica and I are going to San Francisco. Or maybe back to Danville," she announced.

"Is that right?" their father asked.

"What about feeding yourself to a polar bear? Or grizzly?" Nicky joked. She saw her father smile. They didn't usually gang up on Josie, but her sister was being such a pill.

"Yeah. I bet you'd like to watch me get eaten."

Nicky suddenly felt angry at her sister. Marching into the tent, bragging about her new friend, pretending she knew everything about their new home, then saying she wanted to leave the island. They hadn't even arrived! Blinding her father with the headlamp, demanding soup like she was some sort of princess, and poisoning the air with her attitude. She just made everything difficult when things were already hard enough.

If Josie did decide to return to Danville, or go to San Francisco, or travel to India when she turned eighteen, Nicky decided then and there that she wouldn't go with her. It didn't matter that they were twins, or even mirror twins. They'd be apart. And that would be fine.

In fact, thinking about it, maybe she'd never go back to Danville. For her entire life. Just the thought of the fluted limestone columns at the hospital, the hum of the ICU, with the nurses whispering and the computers flashing, made her sick to her stomach. Nicky recalled how her mother raised both palms when she saw Nicky through the glass, making the shape of a heart with her fingers. It was their secret code that she didn't even use for Josie. Mouthing the words *One heart.*

The sick feeling spread up from the pit of her stomach, settling in her throat.

"Time for a joke," their father said, holding out a package of Oreos to them. "Josie, this one's for you. What sits at the bottom of the ocean and frets about everything?"

"A fearful flounder," Nicky said, patting around the tent for her toothbrush and toothpaste. She had a bad taste in her mouth, and she wanted to get out of the tent anyway.

"Close! A nervous wreck."

"You mean a fish named Nicky?" Josie said, laughing as her sister rose to unzip the tent.

Nicky stepped out into the damp ocean wind with a cup of water that she tried not to throw on Josie. She just needed to get away from her sister and breathe.

The rims of her ears turned cold, and the air sliced through her fleece pajamas. She heard Josie saying something to their father, then the woman in the next tent over hummed to her baby. *"Sleep, my little one, sleep . . ."*

Nicky walked to the other side of the boat, wanting to be away from it all. She scanned the black ocean, her eyes picking out a few lights scattered along the coast. Back in Danville, their nighttime ritual consisted of the girls brushing their teeth, then their mother doing a "surgical" sweep of the kitchen, wiping the soapstone counters down with disinfectant, while their father read them bedtime stories. Their mother's deep voice echoed through the halls of their old house in Danville as she called out "Kitchen closed!" Then she climbed the creaky steps to tell stories and sing songs to them before sleep.

As Nicky brushed her teeth, it occurred to her that her father was doing the same thing with the rest of the United

States: closing it down. Cleaning his hands of it. Turning down the lights on Mount Rushmore and Yellowstone, not to mention their life in Danville. Scrubbing it all away, as if it never existed.

Nicky spit toothpaste over the rail, into the night air, wiping her lips with her sleeve. Had he ever asked their opinions? She shivered, her mouth feeling clean and cold. Now she was mad at her father *and* her sister.

She considered going back into the tent for her sleeping bag, which she could hang over her shoulders, so she could continue to look out over the black water, trying to conjure in her head the unknown world below. So much better than dealing with her sister, or even her father with his silly jokes. Then she found herself leaning against the railing, her eyes beginning to shut with exhaustion.

With one last look into the dark, she started back across the deck toward the tent, hoping for a single night of good sleep.

CHAPTER FOUR

Nicky woke to the pitter-patter of rain, and the murmur of the family in the next tent over. She lay there in the half-light with her eyes shut, feeling the shake of the engine along her spine, smelling the salted, piney air. Ocean sloshed against the steel hull.

She turned onto her side and shut her eyes. When she couldn't sleep, she opened them again, and saw just a few leafy strands of hair emerging from the top of her sister's sleeping bag. Nicky pulled herself up and cinched her sweatshirt hood tight against the cold morning air.

The walls of the tent lightened. She checked her father's phone: 5:15 a.m. A text from Aunt Mall. *Y'all make it on the ferry? We'll be there with bells on at the terminal.*

Strange to think of her father having an older sister, with a son of her own. Aunt Mall and Uncle Cliff had visited Danville once, she knew, when Grandpa had died. Nicky was young, and could only recall snippets. Her mother's laugh from across the yard, late at night as her father played guitar and they sang "If I Were a Carpenter" together. The thwack of Uncle Cliff's hammer during the day as he helped build the workshop. Her father over her mother, kissing the top of her head when the roof went up. Even at a young age, Nicky knew this shop was her mother's gift to her father for supporting her all those years as she went through medical school.

Nicky turned to find her father, to see the reassuring shock of his red hair. Her heart flip-flopped when she saw his bag empty. Where had he gone? Then the tent unzipped. Her dad's shaggy, unshaven head burst in. His cheeks glistened with rain.

"Girls! There's a humpback whale!"

A muffled moan came from Josie's corner. Nicky kicked off her sleeping bag, jammed on her flip-flops, and followed him to the railing on the other side of the ferry.

"There!" he shouted, pointing over the water. She focused on the mottled surface of the ocean. The land was closer than it had been last night. Along the dark line of woods she could just make out a dun-colored strip of beach. In front of it, she saw a cone of vapor tear apart in the dim morning light.

"That was the whale breathing. Did you see him?"

"Her," corrected the white-whiskered man she had met the night before, in his wide-brimmed yellow hat. "It's a cow with her calf."

"Oh yeah?" her father said, glancing up.

Nicky met the man's eyes. He winked at her, then directed her gaze back to the ocean with a long, gnarled finger. "There she blows!" he bellowed. "Two of 'em."

Creases of waves rose and flattened out. Nicky knitted her brow, focusing. She was about to look away when the exact spot where he had pointed seemed to unzip. A ridge of muscle emerged, exhaling a burst of misty air. A moment later another ridge broke through the water, narrower and smoother. She sniffed the rich, decaying scent of oily fish and rotting hay, and something else she couldn't identify, insistent and prehistoric—stream banks and turned-over fields and the bottoms of rocks and gardens just before a rain.

"Will you look at all the barnacles on that cow?" the yellow-hatted man shouted.

The sea closed up again, just a gentle boil where the creatures had been. How had the man known where the whales would surface? As the sea filled back in, Nicky thought of the whale and her calf plunging farther and farther into the dark ocean, eyes blinking as salmon and octopus and jellyfish and so many unfamiliar organisms flashed by. She gripped the railing and closed her eyes. So much *wildness* in the cold beneath her.

Flip-flops slapped the wet deck behind her. "What's up?" Josie said, yawning and stretching her arms above her head. "You look like you just touched an electric fence. They're opening the car deck soon. It's your turn to feed Watermelon."

Nicky tried to form words. She wanted to share with her

sister every detail of what she had seen and felt. A mom and her calf. But Josie's pinched, bored expression stopped her.

"We just saw whales," Nicky stammered. "Two of them."

Josie peered out over the wavelets. "I guess I missed the show. I'm going down for breakfast. Meet me in the cafeteria. We can play Uno."

"I'll come with you, J," their father filled in, setting a hand on Josie's shoulder. "I guess if we're up, we're up. I wouldn't mind some Uno. Nick, I'll make you an oatmeal."

Then they were gone. The rest of the crowd dispersed, leaving only the man with the soggy yellow hat. He peeked down the length of the railing and gave her a nod.

"Top o' the morning to you, sailor," he said.

"Good morning. Where's your cat?" Nicky asked.

"Rooster? She don't like mornings, despite her name. Left her in the pickup. Snoozing. She gets a little seasick, too. Hey, sailor?"

"Yeah?" she said.

"Chin up."

Then he slipped between the tents, his long brown boots making not a whisper as he vanished into the sea of fabric.

CHAPTER FIVE

That second day on the boat Josie played games on her phone, or made notes in her journal for her DDF speech. Nicky's father read his guitar magazines and kept returning to the cafeteria to fill up his scarred metal mug with coffee. Nicky stood on deck, her sleeping bag draped over her shoulders, watching as the mountains grew larger, the trees thicker, and the towns along the coast smaller.

The trees, rather than appearing as individuals, like the beeches or maples or oaks on Uncle Max's farm, rolled out in great carpets over the hills. The ocean detonated in white fireworks against the rocks ringing the smaller islands. Nicky squinted north, loving how the salt wind polished her cheeks, stretched out her lungs, and roughened her curls. She only went into the ferry occasionally, for a soup, which she filled at the hot water spigot in the cafeteria, or for a fresh bag of tea. Both she and Josie had started drinking black tea, which their mother had never let them do. She poured in packet after packet of honey, mixing in creamers until she had a small pile of the canisters in front of her. Then back outside, leaning against the railing, sipping the warm liquid, watching the landscape pass.

That second evening, Josie announced she was done with the tent.

"Good luck, homesteaders," she said. "I'm making my own claim."

In the ferry's movie room, she built a nest out of blankets and her sleeping bag beneath one of the Pullman chairs. Nicky stopped by to see her before bed.

"I'm fine," Josie insisted, her headlamp illuminating her book. "The sun just wakes me up too early."

"Are you drinking coffee?" Nicky asked, smelling the grounds, a scent she associated with her mother.

Josie continued to write in her journal.

When Nicky climbed the stairs to the top deck, it was still light outside. Her father wasn't in the tent. A current of panic moved through her. Maybe he had also given up on sleeping outside.

She returned downstairs to the movie room to check with Josie. "Who knows. Maybe he went overboard," she murmured, making a note in her book. The white light flashed in Nicky's eyes. "He's probably playing guitar somewhere."

Nicky returned upstairs. From across the deck she heard the whine of his brass slide, followed by the pluck of a mandolin. Nicky's father slouched in a white plastic chair, his baseball cap pulled low over his eyes, while the man who called her "sailor" stretched out in one of the deck chairs, picking away at the mandolin on his chest.

Nicky stood and listened as the notes carried over the wind. The raindrop sound of the mandolin worked into the tinny drawl of the slide and the deep thrum of the bass notes from her father's resonator guitar.

You know that people are driftin' from door to door,
Can't find no heaven, I don't care where they go. . . .

The brass slide on her father's pinkie finger sparkled in the setting sun. One sad note after another lifted into the night air, while the mandolin, gleaming beneath the glow of the heat lamps, played over top.

Hard time is here everywhere you go.
Time is harder, than ever been before.

In that moment Nicky knew, as clearly as if her mother had whispered it in her ear, that they were traveling north to begin a life none of them could begin to imagine.

CHAPTER SIX

On their last morning, just a few hours from Jackson Cove, Nicky stood on deck, in the corner by the tent, with her sleeping bag slung over her shoulders, sipping tea. She watched as the boat threaded through a series of small islands, some of them no more than rocks tufted with trees. Waterfalls cascaded in long, ragged threads down the sides of mountains. Streams poured from the forests, spreading in tendrils over the crescent-shaped beaches. The rivulets etched themselves into the sand, creating a tangle of waterways that were swept clean by the incoming waves, then filled once more.

Finally the sun broke through the clouds. The top deck grew warm, and people gathered by the railings. Nicky kept her distance, shielding her eyes from the glare on the water, trying to pick out any sign of life between the trees. As they neared Jackson Cove, the land grew closer, the trees almost close enough to touch.

"Look who it is. The Little Sailor."

The man in the floppy yellow hat stood beside her. "Sven Ruger," he said, giving her a quick nod. "Guess I should introduce myself, now that your daddy and I played some music. I'd shake your hand, but, you know, these days . . ." He trailed off.

With her eyes she measured out six feet between them. She had her mask in her pocket, but didn't put it on. He seemed to hear her thoughts and took a step back.

"So, what's your story, sailor? You all on some sort of family adventure? You and your dad and your green-haired sister?"

She paused, unsure about his tone.

"Oh, don't mind me," he went on. "My brother got the talking gift. Me, I'm more used to talking to my cat."

"Me too," Nicky said, surprising herself. "I mean, my sister's better at talking than me."

"That so?"

She nodded.

"You getting off in Jackson Cove?" he asked.

She nodded again.

"You have people there?"

"Aunt Mallory, my dad's sister. And my cousin Clete, and Uncle Cliff."

The man broke into a smile, showing his collection of silver teeth. "Mall's a fun one, ain't she. Got her finger on the pulse. Great big arms. And that son of hers. He's just about the opposite of his old man, who works for the brother I just told you about."

"The one who's good at talking?" Nicky said, looking up at him.

"Good memory. You listen when people talk—more than I can say for my brother. My family came to Alaska about a hundred years back, and started cutting all these big trees. Now my brother's making the case that he should be allowed to cut the valley behind town. Mall's husband, who I guess would be your uncle Cliff, runs the logging crew." The man tipped his hat back, and closed his eyes as light washed over his alabaster skin. "Sun feels good, don't it?"

"Why does your brother want to cut the woods behind town?" Nicky asked.

"Oh, you know," he said, his eyes still shut. "The usual. Money. Big trees back there. There's an old yellow cedar a thousand years old, maybe older. You can see it from town. It'll make a couple hundred garden fences for folks down South, keep dogs from pooping where they shouldn't."

"A thousand years," Nicky said, trying to think back to history class. "That's, like, before Columbus."

"Us white folks were still figuring out how to wipe our butts when that tree was a sapling, probably growing out of a dead log. We call them ghost trees."

"What's a ghost tree?"

"It's a stump that's rotted out from beneath the roots of a sapling. See, the stump nourishes the new tree, then disappears," Sven said, cupping his hand and wiggling his fingers. "You're left with a hollow space at the base of the tree, and roots growing all around it, like the tree has legs and might start walking the next time you turn your back."

Nicky thought about this, trying to recall if she had ever seen a ghost tree on Uncle Max's farm.

"It's particular to the rainforest, as far as I know," Sven said, once more reading her thoughts. "See, trees around here don't go by fire—too rainy. There's not enough soil for trees to roots down into the bedrock. So we get one of our big fall storms, tree goes down, and all those seeds spread about. A few might be lucky enough to fall on a dead log. We call that a nurse log. A tree falls, then spends years soaking up all the vitamins and nutrients from the soil, so it can nurse the saplings like a litter of pups. And that's where the fish come in—it's the salmon that come up the rivers, spawn and die on the riverbanks, then break down so that our soil can be so rich. That's the cycle of life around here. It's how come you see tree roots with nothing beneath them, and trees standing all in a line, standing at attention. Ghost trees, and nurse trees," he concluded, slapping the wet rail in front of him. "See? Who needs school when you got an old teacher like me?"

The idea that trees grew from ghosts and nurses, and dined on salmon, made Nicky's head go light. It was a cool lesson, better than anything Nicky had learned in Danville Middle School.

"So the trees here are carnivores?" she asked.

"Biggest carnivores on the planet since tyrannosaurus! Salmon eat the krill, herring, needlefish, then head back to the streams where they were born to make babies and die. Deposit nutrients in the soil, and the trees grow thick and tall on them. That's how it's been happening way before my

44

people from Norway arrived. Before the Russians. Even before the Tlingit, who've been here for ten thousand years and longer, you want to think about time. Imagine that. Ten of those old yellow cedars, if I got my math right. You and me, sailor, we're just a single square of toilet paper off an entire roll."

Nicky examined the side of the mountain, trying to think of what the earth might have looked like ten thousand years ago, imagining hundreds of fish twinkling in the branches like Christmas tree ornaments.

"Then here comes my brother, wanting to cut it all with his chainsaws. It was our family's mill, but I told him I wanted no part of the operation. We started plundering the forest the day we arrived from Norway. Take a look at that right there, if you want to know what I mean."

Once again Nicky looked at the mountain rising before her. Except this time, instead of seeing the green tips of trees, she saw a field of stumps, with branches scattered about. Each stump about the size of a car. Jagged shreds of bark hung off the stumps, rising into the air. She picked out a few abandoned gas cans, appearing like cherries growing in the tangle. The mountainside looked as if it had been hit by a tornado, a constellation of destruction left behind.

"My cat and me, we do our best to leave a small paw print. But any way you cut it, we're predators. Wired for it. Just like those fish, just like those trees. It's kids like you, and that cousin of yours, who gotta start standing up for these forests. Get ready to be cold, sailor. We're about to slip into the void."

Nicky looked along the side of the boat just in time to see a wall of white cloud coming toward them. The temperature dropped, and the mountain in front of her disappeared from view. Her brow and cheeks went moist. She gripped the cuffs of her sweatshirt and pulled them over her palms, and hugged the sleeping bag to her neck.

The man sighed. "All right, sailor. Older we get, the colder we get—I'm headed inside for coffee. Don't think too much, hear? I'll see you around town."

He gave a short nod and crossed the deck, the cloud swallowing his body, his yellow hat the last thing to go. Nicky heard the hinges of the steel door echo as he went inside.

Nicky peered over the rail, into the whiteness in front of her, thinking of the slashed mountainside. The brightness of the gas cans. Thousands of years of ghost trees, nurse trees, and saplings, fed by fish and rain, all of it cut short by a gasoline-powered steel chain.

The captain came over the intercom. "Jackson Cove coming up, folks—you'll have to take my word for it with this fog! We'll be out of it soon, but there's some liquid sunshine in the forecast. For those of you new to the area, that means rain. For the rest, it means welcome home."

PART TWO

The Arrival

CHAPTER SEVEN

"This feels like one big bad dream," Josie mumbled as their father bent to peel duct tape off the deck with the blade of his knife. Nicky rolled up their tent. "Doesn't where we're staying have a fireplace or something? Don't all houses in Alaska have fireplaces?"

Their father slung his duffel over his shoulder and lifted his guitar. Red and pewter whiskers coated his cheeks. Nicky thought he looked tired.

"Not ours. It's an old miner's apartment, with views of the ocean and forest."

"Do we have to take the stairs again?" Josie moaned.

"All right. I'm sold on your elevator."

She perked up. "Really? You have no logic. You're okay with taking the elevator down, but not up," Josie observed.

He didn't even answer, just marched forward.

When the doors opened onto the car deck, Josie ran over to their camper, unlocked the door, and lifted Watermelon from her cage, nuzzling the iguana's scales with the tip of her nose. Nicky started transferring her dirty clothes from her backpack to her duffel.

"Folks, welcome to Jackson Cove, King Salmon Capital of the World!" the captain announced. "All vehicles disembarking, please do so now."

Engines on the car deck fired up. Their father dropped into the front seat and turned the key. "This is us, girls! It's go time."

Josie set Watermelon back on her rock, and Nicky tossed the rest of her clothes onto her bunk. Their father snapped his magnetic glasses together over the bridge of his nose. A masked attendant gave them an urgent wave, pointing toward the daylight at the end of the boat. "Hurry!" the man shouted.

They weaved among the other RVs, taking the last place in line. "Whew," their dad said. "We almost ended up in Fairbanks."

"Oh my god," Josie said. "Even I know Fairbanks is landlocked. I need coffee. Hey. What's that smell?"

Josie peered back into the camper, where Nicky perched on the edge of her seat in the dinette, waiting for a glimpse of their new home. She was also thinking about ghost trees and nurse logs, and what it might be like to walk through an old forest searching for just things, when she also smelled something. Something burning.

"The heat lamp!" Josie shouted, turning around in her seat. "Nicky, get the T-shirt off Watermelon's bulb!"

Nicky looked down. Clothes were strewn all over, mixed in with the food wrappers and damp towels. Then she saw smoke rising from Watermelon's cage. A flame bloomed, blue at the root. Josie moved past her, pulling the burning T-shirt off the lamp. With her flip-flops she stamped out the flame.

"What is *wrong* with you?" she shouted, her eyes flashing at Nicky. "Would you quit daydreaming for once and join us in the real world?"

"Josie, relax," their father said as they bounced over the steel ramp connecting the ferry to the dock. "The iguana's fine. We're fine. Eyes forward. Who can find Aunt Mall and Clete?"

"She's *your* sister," Josie grumbled, returning to the front seat, cracking a window to allow smoke to escape. "I just wish mine would get her head out of la-la land before something bad happens."

"Who knows. Maybe I won't recognize her. It's been five years since she came back East, when Grandpa died," he said. "Look for a woman with my color hair, standing with a boy your age."

A moist, lemony sea-salt balm seeped into the vehicle, which clunked onto asphalt and started up a short hill to the terminal. A soft drizzle coated the glass. Their father rolled down the window, letting in another smell that made Nicky's nose crinkle—a dank, rotten stench, much worse than burning cotton. Not so different from the smell of whale breath.

"C'mon, girl. You can do it!" their father chanted as he pounded the steering wheel. The engine revved up the incline.

In the front seat Josie cooed, petting Watermelon's head. "You okay, little one?"

As they crested the hill Nicky saw a small crowd in front of the ferry terminal. People wore raincoats, their faces shadowed beneath hoods and baseball caps dark with rain.

"There they are!" their dad shouted, pointing to a tall woman hopping up and down, waving her hands. A boy in jeans and a camouflage coat stood in front of her, tracking their progress.

Aunt Mall pointed to a spot in the lot beside a rusty forest-green pickup truck. The camper stopped with a jolt as their father shoved the gearshift into park.

After hearing her mother talk about "Wild Aunt Mall," Nicky expected a woman dressed in wolf skins with dreadlocks. With a rifle lashed to her back, a collection of foxtails and bear claws strung over her chest.

Instead, Nicky saw that her aunt wore cherry-red lipstick. Her painted fingernails flashed at the tips of her impossibly long, willowy arms. The tall boy beside her wore a brass belt buckle that seemed to hold his gangly body together. Aside from his long frame, he seemed unrelated to his mother, with his red and purple flannel shirt beneath his camouflage coat, and caramel skin. His thick dark hair was pulled into a tight bun. As Nicky looked closer, she saw that he held in his hands a clutch of pink flowers. She recognized her own lean features in the boy, her elongated jawbone and feline eyes, and a certain watchfulness that she instantly understood.

Aunt Mallory pulled open the side door, fluttering her hands.

"Welcome, family! I know your daddy wants you to be cautious, but I'm not hearing another word about social distancing. Y'all get out of this bus this moment and give your old Aunt Mall a hug."

"Mallory, let us at least get a test since being on the boat. I don't think it's safe."

Their aunt shushed their father with a wave of her hand. "I know you all been holed up in this tin can, and we've got not one active case. My nieces need a hug. I can see it in their eyes. Your daddy also needs to a break from this bus—he looks like someone wrung him out to dry. Don't you have a stove in this spaceship? You all need some meat on your bones, you twins need to stand together to even make a shadow."

Josie barely had time to slip Watermelon back into her cage before Aunt Mall snatched her from the front seat into a bear hug. Josie went limp in Aunt Mall's great arms. Her aunt's hair was pumpkin-orange, a few shades brighter than her father's, which Nicky saw now had turned coppery as silver began to work through it.

"Must be five, six years since the last time I saw you two," trilled Aunt Mall. "Your mother had you dressed in some lovely striped twin outfits—in different colors, though. Now what happened here?" Aunt Mall asked, reaching for Josie's hair. "Someone went and dunked you in a vat of green paint. Jackson Cove has a single hairdresser. Even if she's not keeping regular hours we'll get you set up in the chair above her garage. Uncle Cliff's got work to take care of at the mill, with the cut coming up, otherwise he'd be out here to greet y'all. We'll do a salmon dinner tomorrow night out on the island. It'll smell much better than these dying fish you're scenting now. I'm looking for someone else hiding back there in that tin can. Is that little Nicole? Now don't I remember you from when."

Nicky stepped into the light. She saw how the boy hovered behind his mother, inspecting the asphalt. As she came down the steps of the camper he glanced up at her.

Aunt Mall set Josie down and opened her arms to Nicky, who allowed her aunt to gather her up as she came down the steps. At first she resisted the woman's strength. Then the arms squeezed, and she smelled lavender and something else, bark, maybe, woody and strong. After a moment she let her cheek rest against the woman's skin, then relaxed completely, gripping her aunt by her large shoulder blades, which felt like wings, and clutching her.

"Ah, pet. You poor, sweet child. There it is. You just rest. You all have been through so much, and to top it all off, this harebrained trip of your daddy's. I kept telling him to just wrap you in Tyvek and set you on a plane." Her heavy hand raked through Nicky's curls. "Too much for any two girls, really." Nicky could feel her aunt's head shift to look at her father.

Nicky detached from her aunt and met her cousin's eyes. He stared back at her. His eyes were set so deep into his head she couldn't make out his pupils.

"Clete, you planning on giving that fireweed we picked any time soon?" Aunt Mall clucked.

Clete held out the flowers to Nicky. Josie took them, sniffing the petals.

"These smell like weeds," Josie said, laughing. "Did you just pick them from the side of the road? Like, the moment before we got here?"

Aunt Mall laughed too. "Someone's got some sass in her. They say here in Jackson Cove that when the fireweed loses the last of its purple petals, it means summer's over. How many weeks do we have left, son?"

Clete stepped back, seemingly relieved to be rid of his burden. His hands returned to the pockets of his camouflage coat, and he looked down at his brown boots, shiny with the rain.

A rusty old truck growled past. Aunt Mall waved. Nicky recognized Sven in the driver's seat, with Rooster perched on his shoulder. The cat pivoted its head to watch her.

"Grumpy Sven," Aunt Mall said. "The black sheep of the Ruger family. And his trusty cat, Rooster. He's got a house right next to your upstairs apartment."

"Is that right?" their father said. "He can play a mandolin, I'll tell you that."

"It's his rich brother, Lars, who runs the Norseman Mill, where Cliff works," Aunt Mall said. "He's the one who wants to buy up the valley behind town for logging."

"Sounds like that's what everyone's talking about," their father said as he crouched in front of Clete. "Hey, guy. You don't remember me, do you? Your parents didn't bring you along when they came back East."

Aunt Mall watched her son. "Clete, you need to stop looking like the cheese fell off your cracker, and start talking like a person. Doesn't matter if you don't recall your uncle, give him a hug. That's my younger brother."

"Leave the boy alone, Mall," their father said, standing again, but not taking his eyes off Clete. "Those fish jumping out there, you gonna help me catch a couple?"

They all looked over the water, just as two fish almost collided in the air.

"We don't catch humpies," Clete mumbled.

"I'll catch just about any salmon I can get," their father said, smiling. "You're going to have to teach me a thing or two about fishing. We're all used to bass and catfish in Uncle Max's pond. I was always the last to get a bite."

It was true, Nicky thought. Their mother usually had three or four fish in the grass before their father's bobber even twitched. Their mother liked to tease him, giving him a push and saying how lucky he was to have caught her.

"At the moment, Clete's lower 'an a gopher hole because of that Sky River Valley," Aunt Mall explained. "His daddy of course is trying to keep food on our table. Speaking of which, when you come out to the island tomorrow night we'll transform you into real Alaska girls, feed you some salmon and give you some boots. In the meantime, you just forget about this dusty old RV. Forget it like a bad dream. You girls have a real home now. Clete's going to paint you the attic with some blue we've got lying around, and put in some insulation for the winter. I have to say, at this moment the three of you don't look much better than this vehicle, like a chewed piece of twine. Tell me your daddy didn't put you up in that tent on the ferry."

"He did!" Josie yelled, splaying out her hands at the injustice.

"We were just being safe," their father murmured. "If I had my way, we would have stayed in the RV with the iguana."

"Her name is Watermelon. Can we go, Aunt Mall?" Josie asked. "I want to see our new home."

"Of course, darlin'. You got the ocean as a front yard, and miles of forest as your back. You'll be getting a nice deep sleep tonight. Clete, you ride with Nicky here in the pickup. Danny, you follow along, make sure you don't turn that bus of yours into a submarine by driving off the road."

"Why does he keep staring at my sister and me like we just stepped out of another universe?" Josie asked, looking at Clete. "Just because our mother died of the virus doesn't mean we're sick too, okay?"

Aunt Mall's eyes went wide. "Oh, sweetie. Clete doesn't think that."

"Josie, let him be," her father said, taking her shoulder. "Go on, Nicky. You and Clete hop in there."

The hinges on the front door of Aunt Mall's truck screeched. Nicky pulled herself into the cab by the handle.

"There you go. This old rig's nothing but scrap metal, but we only got ten miles of road on the island, so it does us just fine. It *does* have a blower hotter than a burning stump, I'll say that for it. They say the sun might come out tomorrow, but it could be a month. Nicky, those seat belts don't work so well unless you tie them to the clipper, but I wouldn't worry. No one does above thirty around here, for fear of sailing off the road into the ocean. And if we did go for a swim, you wouldn't want to be tied in anyway."

Nicky shifted across the worn bench seat. Clete slipped in beside her as Aunt Mall slammed the door. Then it was just silence. She stared forward as she unzipped her coat. She could feel Clete's eyes on her.

"What?" she finally said. "Why are you staring at me?"

His head snapped back, and he looked down at his hands. "Sorry."

Her cousin reminded Nicky of the white-tailed deer in Pennsylvania. They watched you from the other side of barbed wire, their heads turned almost completely around, desperately curious, with their bodies positioned toward the trees. Ready to bound off at the slightest scent of danger.

Nicky took a deep breath, waiting for Aunt Mall to get in.

"I just want to say that if the virus got real bad, you'd be safe on this island," Clete told her. "People still know how to live off the land. My family has, for thousands of years."

"Okay," Nicky said slowly.

"Did you know there's a spruce in Sweden that's nine thousand five hundred years old? That tree started growing back when people were hunting and gathering."

"That's cool," Nicky said, looking out the window, thinking of the clearcut Sven had shown her just a few hours earlier.

"You know what else?" he said, continuing to watch her.

"What?" she said. If Clete had spoken like this to Josie, she would have bitten off his head.

"I can hear the trees. I'm telling you because I bet you can too."

She turned to her cousin, but before she could answer, the front door opened. Clete didn't blink.

"Nicky, you doing okay, pet?"

As Aunt Mall slid in she put her arm over the bench seat and turned around, her wide hands gripping the upholstery. Despite her upbeat nature, her green eyes, rimmed with eye shadow, appeared watery and concerned. Nicky gave a quick nod. Her aunt turned back to the windshield, but didn't start the truck.

"Your mother's a hero, you know that? She was just about the smartest, most thoughtful person I ever knew, and I can see now she passed it down to you girls. You loved her something awful. Things in Danville go just like clockwork; it's why I ran off to Alaska. I just couldn't abide it." She turned to stare at Nicky. "I have a suspicion you might be an Alaskan girl. You could teach your cousin Clete a thing or two—I keep waiting for him to catch fire."

Nicky glanced at Clete, whose shyness had returned, like cloud cover. The truck frame shook as the engine snarled. They rumbled out of the parking lot, with the camper behind them, and started along the two-lane road hugging the ocean toward her new town.

CHAPTER EIGHT

The following morning Nicky was counting the knots in the unpainted rafters above her head, enjoying the soft mattress—so much nicer than the block of foam in the RV, or her clammy sleeping bag—when Josie rose and started doing yoga. A steady stream of guttural humming emerged from her throat.

"Hey," she called over to Nicky. "Are you awake?"

She came over in her yoga pants and tank top and sat on the edge of Nicky's bed.

"How's the view out the window?" she asked. Nicky rose and they both parted the curtains and set their foreheads against the salt-spotted glass.

Across the blue water, the morning sun hovered above the tree-covered mountains, glinting off the tips of waves. Islands clustered with evergreens speckled the ocean. A fishing boat left a frothy V in its wake as it motored toward the far horizon.

"Whoa! This looks like a postcard. Does this open?" Josie

said, trying to pull up the sash. "Probably all salt-encrusted." She found her phone and started taking photos through the glass.

As Josie fooled with Instagram, Nicky crossed the room and peered out the window over Josie's bed. Just as Aunt Mall had promised, the forest was their backyard.

A valley filled the space beneath the craggy mountains. A few wisps of fog caught in the treetops. Far back, Nicky could see one treetop looming over the others, with a mossy crown. How tall that tree must be—hundreds of feet, she thought. Taller than the geyser at Yellowstone. Taller than any of the oaks or black walnuts in Uncle Max's hedgerows, where deer hunkered down in the fall, hoping they wouldn't be spotted by hunters. The trees only still there because the families who cleared the land had judged the dips, where the sun didn't reach, unfarmable. Instead, they used the hedge-rows as dumps, dragging old farm machinery and hoops from barrels and wheels from carts into the shadows to cor-rode back into the soil.

"Want to switch beds?" Josie called, scrolling through the photos she had taken. "That way you can stare into those trees, and Watermelon can get better light. And I can see the ocean."

"Sure," Nicky said, thrilled at the suggestion. "I'll make your bed if you make mine."

"Deal," Josie said.

Nicky heard voices downstairs and recognized Clete's. Then she heard socked feet on the creaky steps leading up to the attic.

"Hey!" Josie said, pulling the covers to her chin as Clete appeared. "Ever heard of knocking?"

"My mom sent me over to fix the attic for you," he said in a soft voice.

"We can fix the attic ourselves," Josie said.

"You don't have to be so mean," Nicky said as Clete retreated down the stairs. "He's just shy."

"Then you two will be like peas in a pod," Josie said, climbing off the bed and searching for a hair tie. "I can't wait to finally meet up with Veronica. We're going for a walk. She's going to tell me about the totem poles in the park."

"Can I come?" Nicky asked in a small voice.

Josie turned to her. "You know how Mom always said we should tell each other when we see things? Well, I'm sorry to say it, but you've just kind of been a daddy's girl since we left Danville. You don't think for yourself. I don't think you'd get along with someone like Veronica."

Before Nicky could respond, Josie finished putting up her hair, zipped on her fleece, put on her slippers, and disappeared downstairs.

Nicky turned back to the window. That wasn't true. She thought for herself all the time. In fact, that's all she had wanted to do this past month as they hurtled in their RV across the United States: get to a place like this attic where she could stare up at the rafters and think for herself. And a daddy's girl? Maybe she got along better with her dad than Josie did, especially over these last few months. But that didn't make her a *daddy's girl*.

She dressed and went downstairs. Sunlight streamed

through the halls, lighting up the cherry-wood wainscoting along with black-and-white photos of wooden schooners, just their three masts showing above the waves. In the kitchen, their father stood at the counter stirring pancake batter. Clete had a full glass of orange juice in front of him and strummed chords on their father's guitar.

"Hey, kiddo!" their father said. "How was the attic?"

"It smells up there," Josie said, pouring herself coffee.

"I was asking Nicky," their father said. "And J, the coffee was a treat on the ferry. That's your last cup."

Josie laughed. "Okay, dad," she said sarcastically, opening the refrigerator. "Where's the cream? We don't even have milk?"

"Used it all for pancakes," he said. "Sorry."

"Fine," Josie said, seizing her mug. "I'll drink it black, just like Mom."

Nicky examined her father in the Alaska light. Over the course of crossing the country, he had started smiling, even if the smile was crooked, and only came from the corner of his mouth. This morning he smiled fully, at least until Josie mentioned their mother.

"What is that, Clete? 'Three Little Birds'? Sounds good."

"It's a song I made up."

"Really? Nice one."

"Be honest, Clete. The attic smells like rotting mice," Josie said, glancing out the window as she sipped her coffee. "In fact, this whole island seems like a place where humans go to shrivel up and die."

"Josie . . ." Their father sighed.

"What? You can't even tell the difference between morning and night with the sun never setting. It's like some weird limbo the rest of the world has forgotten about."

"Just—please," he said. He gestured toward a mason jar on the table. "Clete was just telling me how, in the spring, the spruce around here make bright new tips. Aunt Mallory and her family collect the tips from their island, and boil them down with sugar to make spruce tip syrup. He brought us over a bottle."

"No kidding," Josie said, lifting the jar and inspecting the handwritten label. "No bottled tree blood for me, thanks. That's like eating babies, and I'm a vegetarian."

Clete stopped playing guitar, sipped his orange juice, and watched Josie. When their father gave him another pancake, Clete tipped the syrup bottle, and the bright red liquid spread over his plate.

"You know, Clete, that's what I used back in Danville, when I made guitars," their father said as he poured the rest of the coffee into a mug. "Sitka spruce. Maybe even from this island."

"Maybe," Clete agreed, cutting his pancakes with the side of a fork. "Though I think all the wood from the Norseman is cut into cants."

"What's a cant?" Josie asked.

"A block of wood. It's what the mill makes, before shipping the lumber off the island."

Their father rested his spoon on the table. "To the Lower 48?" he asked.

Josie scoffed. "You've been here, like, twelve hours, and

already you're talking like an Alaskan. How about 'the continental United States.'"

"Clete," their dad said, sitting down at the table. "What can you tell me about bears in Sky River Valley?"

The smile disappeared from Clete's face. He set down his plate. "As long as you make noise when you're in the woods, you'll be fine. But a lot of them live in there."

Their father considered this. "I guess they'll be hibernating soon."

"Not if the chainsaws wake them up," Josie said. "Veronica told me they could start cutting that forest in just over a week, before school starts. Not this Monday, but next."

"What do you think will happen with the vote? Your mom said people are on the fence," their father asked.

"I don't know," Clete said. "We lost all our tourism money because of the virus. People need jobs, and land to build houses. Most people on the island have at least some association with the mill."

"Is this guy Lars, your father's boss, such a bad dude?"

Clete shrugged. "Dad says he's worked hard to build up the mill after he took control of it, and he's given people jobs. He sponsors baseball teams, and ran the Chamber of Commerce. He gave us wood to build our cabin."

"He sounds like someone who cares about making sure people have jobs," their father said.

"Fishing is a job, isn't it?" Josie interrupted as her father dropped a pancake onto her plate. She picked up her knife and started to saw through it. "Seems like you self-quarantine on your boat. That's what Veronica and I are going to talk about today, for her speech to town on Wednesday. She should be here any minute."

Clete turned to her. "Veronica Deschumel?"

Josie nodded.

"How do you know her?" he asked. "And what do you know about fishing?" Suddenly he didn't seem so shy.

Josie sat up, obviously taken aback by his tone. "We learned to fish in Pennsylvania. With my mom and her brother, at his pond," Josie responded. "And Veronica's the head of DDF. Don't you know that?"

"Yes," he said evenly. "Her parents came from Seattle a few years ago. Her mother's from Metlakatla and is Tsimshian. Mr. Deschumel runs Jackson Cove Convos. They live on Janie's Alley, out on the road toward the mill."

Josie nodded. "We're talking about the same person. I did my tryout speech for her on this topic, about how we shouldn't touch the earth for the next one hundred years, and Veronica said it was awesome. Then she asked if I could help her with her speech this Wednesday at the town hall."

"What do you mean, not touch the earth?" Clete asked, an edge growing in his voice. "What about, like, walking on it?"

Josie paused, then smiled. Nicky could see that Josie hadn't expected a fight this morning, but was more than happy to engage. There was nothing Josie liked more than a good debate.

Their father rose to flip a pancake, and Nicky took his seat, prepared to kick Josie under the table if she needed to.

"What if people can't find other jobs?" Clete said. "I mean, we don't just fish and hunt for food up here. Most things arrive on a barge from Seattle. There are no cows, for example. People need money for milk."

Josie's wooden chair creaked as she sat back. Nicky knew she was considering her angle of attack. "People here on your island will chop down the trees, take the fish, dig the gold, until there's nothing left. That's what people do. They're really no better than termites. Unless agitators like Veronica and I speak out against people like you, and your father, break the trend, then extraction will continue. We need to change the will of others, to make them understand."

Clete shook his head. "My dad taught me how to cut down a tree at the age of five, so we could put a roof over our heads and warm ourselves in winter. I've grown up watching him at the mill. He built that house out of trees we processed together. People on this island depend on wood. We live in a forest, after all."

"That's exactly my point!" Josie said. She set her slippers on the floor and leaned forward. Nicky nudged her shin, but Josie just moved her legs away. "Someone has to stop you Alaskans, because you obviously can't stop yourself."

Nicky's father butted in. "Josie! You need to watch your tone."

"What. You think I should speak politely while the world burns? While everything I'm supposed to 'inherit' disappears?"

Clete swallowed another drink of orange juice, smiling

at Josie's air quotes. He narrowed his eyes, focusing on her. "So you don't think we should ever cut down a tree? What about the chair you're sitting in?"

"No," Josie said, unscrewing the lid of the spruce-tip syrup, smelling it, and making a face. "I think the earth has been through enough. It needs to convalesce. That means to recover, like you recover from being sick. *If* we even *ever* recover. It might all be a lost cause. Trust me, if I could live somewhere other than this apartment, a place where things weren't made out of wood, I gladly would."

"Okay, okay," their father said. "We get the point, J."

"What about Uncle Max?" Nicky asked. If she couldn't kick her sister beneath the table, she decided she'd just take Clete's side. "He cuts hay and corn. People here cut trees. What's the difference?"

Josie flashed her a look, then reached across the table to chop off a pat of butter. Nicky hardly ever took on her sister, at least in a debate.

"You're right, Nicky. It *is* the same idea. The same thing that humans have been doing for ten thousand years. Specifically, white men. Go somewhere, destroy the land, repeat. Except the moment has come when people like me realize we either keep doing this until we kill ourselves, or we stop. Uncle Max's land is already spent. You know that better than anyone, with all the time you spend wandering around up there. He grows corn, soy, hay. True, you'll say, there are those trees, beeches and oaks and maples that Uncle Max probably would have cut down to send his kid to college

68

like the rest of the farmers in Pennsylvania, except he didn't have kids. Or to buy a new pickup, a snowmobile, whatever."

"We call them snowmachines in Alaska," Clete said.

"I'm not Alaskan," Josie shot back. "In fact, I shouldn't even be living on this island, considering that it was stolen from Indigenous people. But I'm here, and I'm going to do everything I can while I am to work with Veronica to empower others."

"Why not do that for Pennsylvania?" Clete asked.

"Pennsylvania's done for. Mowed over. It's too far gone for anyone to make a difference. So is the rest of the United States, from what I've seen over the past three weeks. Sure, we make ourselves feel good by recycling our plastic, or using LED light bulbs. Maybe we use laundry detergent that won't kill frogs in the Susquehanna River. But who are we kidding? Yellowstone, and the rest of the national parks in the country, are becoming open-air museums. We saw it for ourselves at the geyser. Look, but don't touch. There's still a chance in Alaska. There's still hope."

"I agree, at least with some of what you're saying," Clete said slowly. "But I think you need to consider that you just arrived on an island where people have been existing for ten thousand years. You can't just tell others what to do. I mean, you might have good intentions, but you don't know the details."

Josie pushed her plate away. "Apparently I have to, because no one on this island except Veronica and maybe the rest of DDF understands."

"Josie, you are being disrespectful to your cousin," their father said. "You need to apologize."

"Give it a rest with the Dad-in-charge voice," Josie said, rising from the chair and grabbing her coffee mug. "It's not like you have better answers. You dragged us all the way to this island, and now that we're here, we're just as lost as we were in the beginning." Josie brushed past their father, then turned to stand in the doorframe. "The truth is, we always will be lost, because it was Mom who gave us direction. Without her, we're bouncing around like a bunch of free electrons."

"That's so not true," their father whispered.

Josie tromped down the stairs. "I'm going to Totem Park with Veronica!" The door slammed behind her.

After a moment their father faced the sink and turned on the water. Then he just stood there.

"I can help, Uncle Dan," Clete said quietly.

He gripped the hot and cold knobs, as if for balance. Water splashed up from the dishes. To Nicky's surprise, her father turned away from the running water, lifted his guitar from the couch, and left the kitchen. Nicky listened for the creak of the stairs as her father went outside to look for Josie. Instead, she only heard the moan of the hinges as the door shut, followed by a few notes as her father began to play another sad song.

CHAPTER NINE

Nicky stood in front of the sink, running a finger through the water and adjusting the knobs. She handed Clete a kitchen towel. "I'm sorry for my sister. I think she misses her friends. And, we all miss our mom."

"I know," he said, stepping aside. "Having your life changed by this virus must be hard. And your mother . . ." His voice drifted off.

Nicky set the glasses above the sink. "Sometimes I think she's having a harder time than me, or even Dad. She's just not open to much."

Clete nodded. "Your dad's cool. He made that guitar?"

"He had a shop. Your dad helped him build it, when I was seven."

"I remember that. My mom and dad left the island for Grandpa's funeral. I was seven too. I hadn't even met my grandfather. I guess he never really forgave my mom for coming to Alaska and marrying an Indian. My mom told me that that's what Grandpa called my father."

Nicky reached for the detergent to wash the cast-iron pan. "It sounds mean, but you didn't miss much. He was always kind of cranky, though I liked his stories. We only saw him every now and then."

Clete gently took the pan from her, sloshed water around it, and set it on the stove, pouring in a dash of olive oil.

"Best to just rinse, and season," Clete said. "Soap ruins it."

"Dad took us to see him sometimes," Nicky continued. "He found quarters in our ears, and made Styrofoam bunnies disappear. At the funeral I remember your mom crying."

When she looked at him she could see that he was trying to imagine his tough, loud mother in tears.

"Maybe we should go up and paint the attic before your twin gets back," he finally said, taking a paper towel to wipe down the cast-iron pan, which had grown shiny with heat.

"Okay. Don't let Josie scare you. Lately I don't even think she likes me."

"She doesn't scare me," he said as they walked through the hall, guitar music coming from her father's room. "I think she's just really sad."

"Probably. Hey," Nicky said as they climbed the stairs to the attic. "Want to help me move this tank? Josie and I are switching beds."

"Sure."

Nicky unplugged Watermelon's heat lamp and took one side. Watermelon's head twitched as his home shifted yet again.

"You're definitely getting the better view," Clete said. "At least until they cut down the trees."

Nicky climbed over the bed and set her forehead against the window. The fog had burned off, and she could see clear to the back of the valley, where the mountains started.

"I can't believe that actually might happen."

Clete joined her at the glass, kneeling on a pillow and looking out.

"You see that lighter-colored treetop there, about half-way up the valley?" Clete asked. "The tall one?"

She picked out the frilly point she had noticed that morning. "I see it."

"My dad says it's been living for over a thousand years. They call it the Old Yellow Cedar."

"That old fisherman, Sven, told me about it on the ferry," Nicky said.

"Did he tell you about the Three Guardsmen?"

Nicky shook her head.

"There are two big hemlocks and a spruce in front of the cedar. They poison the soil around them, so they can be alone. It's called allelopathy. I think of them as cranky trees, because they stand tall on the far side of the river, protecting the Old Yellow Cedar."

"My uncle planted a forest of Norway spruce on his farm when he first arrived," Nicky said.

"Planted forests never get big, because the trees aren't connected underground. The trees just end up fighting for nutrients beneath the soil. In Sky River Valley, the trees are all linked up by mushrooms. Fungal threads connect them, growing between their roots. It's how they communicate, the mother trees providing the saplings with nutrients, the Three Guardsmen clearing the soil around the cedar."

"I never knew that," Nicky said.

"Trees can even warn each other about predators by releasing scent in the air. And that's just the beginning. There's so much we don't know about them, especially old-growth, like in Sky River Valley."

"What do mushrooms get from helping trees?" Nicky asked, recalling from biology the word *symbiotic*.

"The fungi get carbohydrates from the roots. In exchange, the trees use the network built by them, which people call the Wood Wide Web. It's all just about the opposite of a Christmas tree farm."

Nicky slid off the bed and began to make it. She had never thought of Uncle Max's forest of Norway spruce as a bunch of trees boxing each other beneath the soil, or of Christmas tree farms as anything other than neatly ordered cones planted along hillsides waiting for the holiday.

"How well do you know Sven Ruger?" Nicky asked. "I met him on the ferry."

"Old Sven. No one knows him that well. He and his cat kind of keep together. My mom once wrote an article in the *Courier* about how he plays mandolin to the fish. Rooster meows along. That's why they catch so many."

"He told me about nurse trees, and ghost trees, and how the trees are carnivores," Nicky said as Clete shook out a canvas drop cloth. With his pocketknife he popped open a can of paint, then mixed it with a stick.

"Pretty cool, right?" Clete said. "When you come to our island tonight, I'll show you a line of saplings that grew up from a nurse log."

"Okay," she agreed, watching as he poured blue paint into a metal tray.

He looked up at her. "You know, I wasn't kidding when I said in the car that I could hear the trees."

Nicky dipped a brush into the tray, wiping it along the edges.

"I didn't think you were," she said. "Where should I start painting?"

"The rafters," he said.

He seemed to sense that she preferred silence, and they got to work. She painted the wide-open spaces first, just like Uncle Max had taught her. Clete used a roller, steadily filling in the knee walls before he switched to a brush. He flung the work cloth over Josie's bed, his brow knitting as he painted the sides and undersides of the rough-hewn rafters. With his pocketknife he started cutting rectangles of insulation, the foam squeaking as it slipped on the wet paint.

"Your sister can touch things up later," he said. "Even though she doesn't seem to care about details."

Nicky laughed, both at his joke, and the idea that Josie would ever pick up a paintbrush. "I wouldn't worry too much about her."

When all the rafters were painted, she set down her brush in the tray.

"I like trees," Nicky started. "I've always liked them. I

read about them, and go walking all the time on my uncle's farm. But they're just—trees. Even though I sometimes wish they could talk, I also know they can't."

Clete stood with a piece of insulation in one hand. "You mean you've never heard them?"

"No," she said definitively.

"I'm not talking about like in some Disney movie," Clete said, smiling. "It's not like you're in the woods and they start waving their branches, swaying and making *oooh* sounds. Like I said, they communicate through the soil, and also through the air. In biology class we learn that they're all battling to grow the highest, competing for the most sunlight. It's more complicated than that. They're helping each other, especially the old-growth valleys, like the one out your window. They're a family. Old trees blow down, new ones grow in their place. It just happens at such a slow pace that we hardly notice, because our lives are too short."

Nicky didn't respond. Clete tore open a new package of rollers, tossing her one. "Why is that such a crazy thought? A mother tree blows a lucky seed onto an old stump, and that stump keeps the seed out of the snow, nourishing the sapling as it grows. When it connects into the fungal network, the mother tree feeds it nutrients through the filaments, helping the sapling grow. Humans take care of their young. Why not trees?"

"Because they're like fish—they have thousands of seeds. I don't see salmon out there nursing their babies."

"Of course salmon nurse their babies. After a salmon dies, it washes up on the bank and rots, creating nutrients for bugs to grow. Salmon fry eat the bugs when they hatch in the spring. You're just not thinking about it in the right way."

A shiver moved through Nicky as Clete said this. Even after they died, salmon helped their children.

"When you touch a tree, it's like feeling a heartbeat through someone's chest, or touching a live wire and getting a shock."

"That's not the same as talking."

"That's all talking *is*," Clete insisted. "Sending signals." With his knife he pointed out the window toward the valley. "Those trees out there, they're talking right now. You know what about?"

A buzz started at the base of Nicky's spine, spreading over her back. She held his stare. "What?"

"They're talking about *you*."

"No," she said, shaking her head. "Maybe you didn't hear me. Trees don't talk, and they *definitely* can't tell the difference between people. And once animals are dead, they're dead. That's it. It's just that simple."

"They knew you were coming," Clete continued, punching in a piece of insulation with a closed fist. "That part I don't get. I mean, I understand the mycorrhizal network—trees connected by millions of miles of filament built by mushrooms beneath the soil. The soil is alive in the same way the ocean is—thousands of terrestrial insects down there working together to stabilize the ground cover, and help the trees. Why don't we study the soil like we study the sea? But the hemlocks and cedars and spruce on the island where I live—where you'll come tonight—those trees actually knew you were coming. I guess it's not *that* weird, considering they use scents and signals through the network to warn of insects, and disease. But a person?" He closed his utility knife and turned thoughtful. "Signals can't travel through the ocean. It's gotta be a scent, though the sea winds would have blown it off. I don't know. Maybe a mushroom that floated on a current . . ."

Nicky stepped toward him, her hands on her hips. It was all too much. "If you keep saying trees talk I'm going to stomp out of here just like Josie did."

Clete watched her, working to read her face to see if she was serious. Then he leaned down to slice a batt of insulation. "Nicky, the network beneath the soil is lit up like a Christmas tree. Everyone—all the trees—are alive with it. A signal went out the moment you stepped foot on the island."

Blood rushed in her ears. None of this made sense. "Me? I don't know anything about this island. What are they saying?"

With an open palm he pounded insulation into the space between the rafters. "Simple. They said you're the one who's going to save them."

"Save them from what?"

He ran his marker down another rectangle, making a neat black line, then picked up his knife. It hovered in the air like a wand. "From me, Nicky," he said softly. "From Lars Ruger, the owner of the Norseman Mill. From my father. Your sister was right—from this island."

Clete started across the room for another piece of pink insulation. His words echoed off the attic ceiling.

"It doesn't matter if you don't believe me. You'll find out soon enough. Soon everything I'm telling you will make sense."

CHAPTER TEN

L ater that afternoon Nicky stood on the boardwalk outside their house, waiting for Josie and her father to
come down the stairs. Uncle Cliff had said to meet him
at the harbor and they'd take a skiff out to the island where
smoked salmon, salmon dip, baked salmon, pickled salmon,
and salmonberry pie, with salmonberries on top, awaited.

Nicky tightened the straps on the life vest her father had
given her until it fit snugly around her shoulders. Nothing like the clunky orange thing her mother had made her
wear when they fished from a canoe on Uncle Max's pond,
even though the shore was just a couple swim strokes away.
Her mother had been so careful, sequestering herself in the
opposite end of the house, using a hot plate as a kitchen,
to keep them safe. *Why hadn't she done the same with herself?*
Nicky wondered. She was so smart—surely she must have
understood that, if she got sick, then their father would be at
a loss for how to take care of them. Had she decided, using
her logic, that saving strangers was more important than

keeping her family together? It was all too much to think about.

Clouds loomed above the mountains. The weather came in so fast. It was hard to imagine that she had woken up to a bluebird day, not a cloud in the sky, and now she couldn't see the sun.

Clete had left just after noon, skiffing back to help his father cut wood. She couldn't believe what he had told her, that she was some sort of "chosen one" the trees had been expecting. Maybe, she thought, after growing up in these forests, Clete could detect some mode of communication, but for him to hear that the cedars and spruce and hemlocks were *waiting* for her—he must have read too many fantasy books. She probably would have done the same if she had grown up on an island off yet *another* island in Alaska, though her mother never would have let that happen. "We don't run away from our problems, Nicky. Problem, solution. Problem, solution. It's just a matter of keeping calm, and searching for the answer. It's what I do every day in the ER. We figure out what the medical problem is, and find a treatment. It's always out there, just waiting for us to find it."

Instead, Nicky took to reading her fantasy books during free periods at school. From Frodo to Katniss Everdeen to Edward Tulane, she loved how these characters daydreamed and had the courage to step away from the real world to meet their destinies. Even though she felt it was almost betraying her mother, she knew that this was how her mind worked.

It felt good to have discovered a family member her age

who also loved the woods. Usually it was Josie who made friends quickly—and she had, with Veronica—but Nicky felt easy around Clete. Veronica intimidated her, with her generous smile and easy confidence. Still, Nicky wished Clete would stop making up stories about the trees having conversations about her beneath the soil.

She pushed these thoughts from her mind, stepped onto the gravel road, and tipped her head back so she could see the roof of their house, with its weathered gray shingles. She picked out the faded red-gabled dormer where she slept. Through the glass she could see the rafters she and Clete had painted blue, with the pink insulation stuffed between them.

The miner's house where they now lived was just about the opposite of their royal blue Victorian off Main Street in Danville, with its wraparound porch and stained-glass windows, and white picket fence in the back separating it from the Presbyterian church where her grandfather had preached. Their parents had spent hours steaming off wallpaper, sanding the wooden floors, and polishing the curved banisters, restoring their father's childhood home.

When Uncle Cliff and Aunt Mall came back for Grandpa's funeral, Nicky remembered Aunt Mall marveling at all they had accomplished. While Aunt Mall packed up Grandpa's things at the house where he had lived, just down the street from the church, Uncle Cliff helped her father build a guitar workshop in the elms, stringing the mahogany platform in front with lights. Nicky somehow knew her father had always wanted to do this, and yet hadn't been able to while his own father lived. She recalled waking up to the sound of Aunt Mall and Uncle Cliff and her mother singing along as their father strummed "Sweet Caroline" on one of his shiny resonator guitars. Her mother seated, laughing as she threw back her head, breathed deeply, and belted out the words.

Over the years their father had taken to spending less time teaching guitar, and more time in his shop. He started selling a few guitars to people in Williamsport. There had been calls from Philadelphia, and even New York City. "No one can make a guitar that cries like your father's," their mother told them. "I promised you," she said to him, quoting their song, "if you were a carpenter, I'd still have your babies."

She only really joked like this around their father. With everyone else—even Nicky and Josie—she remained serious. When Josie threw up after a double scoop of Birthday Cake ice cream following a baseball game, their mother was the one in the bathroom wiping her lips with a damp towel, pushing a pressure point on her inner arm to stop nausea, telling her how she had to know her own limits. She was the one rubbing Nicky down with oatmeal soap when she got poison ivy at Uncle Max's, covering her in calamine lotion. When their father got home from his administrative job at the hospital, he usually showered, slipped into his jeans, and went out to his workshop, where he turned his blues music on loud and got to what he considered his real work, the work he loved.

While Josie went on about her day to their mother,

Nicky often visited her father. She couldn't get enough of the gummy scent of freshly glued guitars, hanging in neat rows from the rafters. Out the window you could see the great oak on the lawn of the Presbyterian Church, where Grandpa said the British camped during the Revolutionary War. The oak had crooked, gnarly branches that Nicky and Josie had climbed as kids, the two of them finding their own reading spots—Nicky's high up, Josie's just off the ground. They'd sit in the tree, glancing up from their books in the evening, waiting for their mother's shiny pickup to return from Geisinger Medical Center. Then they'd scamper down and dash through the tangle of bushes past the workshop, Nicky pausing to shout through the open window, "Mom's home!" Then she'd charge across the lawn to catch up with Josie, knowing that she never would, because Josie was in a full-out sprint to meet her mother's embrace.

As hard as Mom worked in the ER, when she pulled into the driveway and shut down her pickup, her mind was devoted completely to her girls—listening to Josie's report on which teachers she did and didn't like, and to Nicky's adventures with Sonya or her stories about baling hay on Uncle Max's farm.

What struck Nicky as funny was that their father kept repeating to them as they crossed the country to take no chances. Sterilize everything. What was *he* thinking, bringing them to a remote island in Alaska where he didn't even have a job? From that cozy house they knew so well to this rickety old building, built by some gold miner desperate to make his fortune. None of it made sense.

A gravelly voice broke her from her thoughts. "Hey, sailor. You expecting a flood to pass through?"

Nicky looked up to see Sven leaning against his truck, one foot propped on a tire. His camel brown boots were folded over at the ankles, covered in nicks. He ran a hand across Rooster, who stretched out along his wrist.

"That must be a gift you have, just to disappear into your thoughts like that." Before Nicky could reply, he said, "You catch any shut-eye on that ferry? Rooster, she don't sleep much on boats. Neither do I, really. Never could." The cat purred lazily, watching Nicky with golden eyes.

Nicky squinted at him. "My aunt said you're a fisherman."

"Oh sure. That's why we don't sleep. Too busy catching fish."

"Do you catch a lot?"

He smiled down at her. "That's why they call it *fishing* and not *catching*. Never know what'll happen when you head out onto the water."

She heard footsteps, and watched as her father and Josie emerged from the apartment. Josie's green ponytail flopped out of the back of her purple Ironmen mesh cap. Her father wore his favorite pair of jeans.

"What are you doing standing in the street?" her father asked, resting a hand on her shoulder and turning to Sven. "Evening."

Sven broke into a smile. "Evening, guy. *Senorita*," he said, bowing to Josie, who shrank back. "Guy, I been wanting to ask since we played on the ferry. Where'd you buy your instrument?"

"I built it," their father said, glancing down the road.

"Is that right? Well. Those notes, I couldn't get them from my head. Haunting, like you could call up the dead with that music."

"I'm sorry," their father said, stepping back. "We're supposed to meet someone on the docks."

"Oh, I don't mean to hold you up." He stopped petting the cat and reached out his hand. "We played music, but I don't think we met. Sven Ruger."

Their father didn't move. "I don't mean to be unfriendly, Sven, but as you know, we just came up on the ferry."

"Of course. Take no chances, right?" the man said, winking at him and retrieving his hand. Nicky felt her father's hand tighten on her shoulder. "Me and your daughter had a nice powwow about trees up on the top deck. She knows more than she thinks she does. I better git. Good evening to y'all."

Her father watched the man walk away. He looked down at Nicky. "Did he say anything to you?"

"No," Nicky said, annoyed. "We were just talking."

"He looks scary," Josie said. "That tomcat's creepy."

"Rooster's a she," Nicky corrected.

"Well, then, maybe she's a witch. Those golden eyes give me the willies."

"C'mon. We'll miss Uncle Cliff," their father said, starting down the hill toward the harbor.

Josie held a notebook in her hand. It astonished Nicky that her sister got frightened by talking to one old man, and yet had the courage to get up in front of people she didn't know and make a speech.

Rigging in the boats banged and clanked in the wind. Tree-covered mountains rose at steep angles behind the masts. Nicky stared across the water, imagining two thousand grizzly bears parading beneath the tree canopies, like whales below the ocean surface. Huge, quiet, and unseen. Nicky was surprised when she felt Josie's hand take her own as they reached the sidewalk.

"So who's ready for SalmonFest 2020?" their father said, oblivious to the girls holding hands, and obviously trying to lift the gloom that had set over them.

"Me," Nicky said, wanting him to just stop talking so this moment with her sister could last.

The evening felt like one in Danville, when they'd all be walking along the Susquehanna, holding purple banners, turning up Main Street to the Forge for a burger before watching the Ironmen play Bloomsburg at the diamond along the water. One of her mother's favorite things to do. She'd stand in the bleachers and scream at the thwack of the bat, cupping her hands over her mouth to yell the hitter's name. She knew the entire high school team's roster. Nicky and her father would exchange embarrassed glances, while Josie would get up and scream beside her mother.

People in town joked about that. No team had a fan like Dr. Hall. After baseball games they'd go out for Turkey Hill ice cream. Dad would get Graham Central Station, his favorite, Mom a single scoop of Moose Tracks with chocolate sprinkles, and Josie and Nicky Birthday Cake with rainbow sprinkles. "I swear I can hear all that sugar rushing through your veins," their mother would say.

The summer before, when life was normal, their mom had coached their softball team, leaving the hospital early to meet the girls at the batting cages. Taking them all on a trip to the Little League World Series in Williamsport. Throwing endless pop flies and grounders until it got too dark to see the ball. Even then, Josie would want more.

"Hey, Dad. Seems like a night for a baseball game, doesn't it?" Josie said in a small voice, and she gave Nicky's hand a squeeze. Their father, lost in thought, peered out over the water. He didn't seem to hear her. Without thinking, Nicky squeezed her sister's hand back.

Maybe Estelle Parisi Hall wouldn't have liked sleeping on the deck of the ferry, or even sleeping in an RV. But Nicky could see her mother by the harbor, closing her eyes and breathing this air deep into her lungs. She'd like the adventure of setting off on a skiff for a salmon dinner on an island. She had always said she admired Aunt Mall, even if she thought she was a bit wild. If she were here tonight, they would have all been holding hands as they walked down to the harbor. She wished her father would agree with Josie, and tell them this.

Her mother had been so difficult to predict. She either wanted to be at the hospital, in the frenzy of the emergency room, tending to farmers who had had their arms chewed while reaching into a combine to free a cornstalk, or at home, tending to her rhododendrons with her clippers, and keeping her kitchen clean of grease. Or she wanted to go to baseball games, and eat ice cream with the family, folding her napkin neatly around her cone so her fingers wouldn't get sticky.

That was the most difficult part, Nicky decided as she walked. The emergency room gave her mother adventure, but also the ability to stitch things up and make them whole again. Her mother always found a solution. Even after Estelle got sick, and left the house for the hospital, Josie insisted that her mother would cure herself—and also the rest of the world, by finding some magic cure for Covid-19, and all the variants that might pop up.

Their father stopped walking, and crouched to look them in the eyes. He smelled of spiced aftershave and soap, rather than the usual comforting, tired odor of his pressed shirts and khakis that he wore to the hospital. "Girls, I want you to know —"

Josie pulled her hand away from Nicky. "Dad. We know. You love us."

He stared at her. "I do. I also wanted to tell you—you're getting old enough to hear these things—that Aunt Mall and Grandpa didn't always get along. But she's a great woman. You should have seen her on the basketball court—there are still pictures of her at Danville High. She was a power forward, long and strong. She could have played in college if she hadn't come out here to work for a summer, and ended up staying. In fact, I think you girls have some of her in you. I know she's not your mother, but a loving aunt is good for both of you."

"Whoa!" Josie said, interrupting her father. "You're already wanting to replace Mom with your sister?"

"That's not what I'm saying, Josie."

A bird flew overhead, its broad wings making a whooshing sound as they beat the air. "That's an actual bald eagle!" Nicky yelled.

"It is," their father said, watching as the bird flew out over the ocean.

"Probably shouldn't take Watermelon for a walk," Nicky said.

"Not funny," Josie snapped. "Plus, I don't think an eagle would eat an iguana."

"Why not?" Nicky countered. Josie talked so much about nature and the environment, and yet she hardly ever stepped outside. "Eagles eat fish. Salmon. Watermelon's just like a big green fish, except with four stubby legs. Ask Veronica. I bet she'll tell you the same thing."

"Veronica doesn't waste her time wandering around the woods. She knows every symbol on the totem poles in the park. She's focused on getting straight As, and wants to go to an Ivy League college. I bet Clete doesn't even like to read."

"What does Clete have to do with it?" Nicky asked. The hand that had held Josie's burned. "He's your cousin too."

"Enough. Just—enough from both you," their father said. "Each time I try to treat you like adults . . . Can you just help me find Uncle Cliff's skiff? He said to look for a blue canopy. I think I see it."

They were turning toward the ramp when a car slowed

beside them. A middle-aged woman with wisps of gray hair pushing out of her blue handkerchief jammed her palm on the horn.

"Hey! Aren't you the family from back East?" she said from beneath her mask, which showed a big red salmon.

Their father stopped walking. "Pennsylvania," he said, lifting his own mask over his mouth.

"Well, you're supposed to be in your house, do you know that? Not walking around spreading the virus." She turned to the girls. "You two don't even have masks."

He stepped forward. "We got tested before coming here. We *are* in quarantine, but taking a walk."

"I'm the mayor of this town," the woman said, picking up her phone. "If you were in quarantine, you'd be back in that house of yours on top of the hill."

Their father stepped forward. When he spoke, his tone surprised Nicky. "Go on. Throw us off the island. You think I care?"

Nicky heard footsteps coming up the ramp.

"Alice, it's fine," a man said, hustling toward them. "Danny, please. Alice is just doing her job. Alice, I was taking my brother-in-law and my nieces out for a bite of salmon on the island. Go on, now. They tested before arrival, just like the regulations say. No need to worry. Everything's safe."

They hadn't found Uncle Cliff—Uncle Cliff had found them.

CHAPTER ELEVEN

Nicky's brightest memory of Uncle Cliff was him on a ladder, holding nails between his teeth as he hammered shingles. She remembered his wide shoulders and his bushy moustache that cast shadows over his lips—the same one he had now. Like Clete, he dressed in a flannel and jeans, though he wore no belt. Steel shined through the toes of his scarred XtraTuf boots.

The woman who had just been yelling at them set down her phone and eyeballed their uncle, who now stood with them. "We're on an island, Cliff. You know that better than the rest of us. I'll see you at the town hall next week."

"Probably before, Alice."

The woman drove off. Uncle Cliff turned to their father and hugged him. "Oh man. I'm sorry about that, brother. What a way to be welcomed. Alice, she takes the job of mayor way too seriously. And the rest of it . . . it's just so, so sad. I wish we coulda flown East this summer. But you know, with the virus, and the tickets, and plane travel . . ."

Nicky and Josie looked on as the two men gripped one another. When their father finally let go, Uncle Cliff continued to hold him by the shoulders.

"It's just good to be here," their father said. "Girls, you remember your uncle? He used to throw you into the clouds. He helped me build my shop, just after your grandfather died."

"We'll just have to build you another once you get settled," Uncle Cliff said.

He had the same deep-set eyes as Clete, except Uncle Cliff's were weathered, creased at the edges. His irises were lighter and sun-splattered. Kind eyes, Nicky thought as she watched him kneel and open his arms. Nicky couldn't help herself. She hugged him around the neck. When she pulled away she found wood shavings stuck to her sweatshirt.

"That's good luck," he said. "Cedar dust and herring scales. Means you'll be finding more of what you need."

Josie hung back, and gave a short wave. "Hi."

"Hiya, Josephine. I guess you're probably old enough now for me to call you that. You girls ready for a ride? Looks like one of you already has her life vest on," he said, nodding at Nicky with approval.

They filed down the ramp. An aluminum boat that swooped up into a point at the front knocked against the dock. Fishing rods stood up in metal holders. A blue canvas cover was fastened to the bow of the boat, where Uncle Cliff directed them.

"You girls just settle right beneath that spray skirt," he

said. "Get those vests clipped on tight. I'll try to find us some otters, and maybe a whale on the way out."

With the toe of his boot he pushed the boat off the dock. They motored toward the rocky opening of the harbor, where a green light and a red light blinked on either side of the entrance. "That's port, and that's starboard," he said, pointing at the green light. "So boats can get home at night."

"Cool," Nicky said.

"Prepare for warp speed!" Uncle Cliff shouted as the engine roared to life. Nicky gripped the poles of the console, and her father held on to the railings as Uncle Cliff pushed the throttle forward. The boat evened out as they accelerated, the ocean whizzing past on either side. Salt-spray coated her cheeks as they bounced over waves. Beyond the runway of the airport the volcano slipped into view. The sky behind it was trimmed with a band of amber, just above the sun, which had reappeared near the horizon.

"Josie!" Nicky yelled into the canvas cover, her heart beating. "You need to see this. It's the most beautiful thing ever, like another world."

Josie lay in a pile of flotation pillows and rope, her eyes open but her body not moving.

"This view would get 250 hearts on Instagram, I bet," Nicky said. Josie only shook her head.

"'Red sky at night, sailor's delight. Red sky in the morning, sailors take warning.' Isn't that what they say?" their father asked Uncle Cliff.

Cliff laughed. "I grew up on this island and I still can't

94

tell what the heck the weather's about to do. They call it the Inside Passage, but we're actually on the Outside. That's why our fish are so bright and our trees so big. Conditions always changing. There!" he said, swerving the boat to port. "Look. Sea otter."

Nicky followed Uncle Cliff's finger. A slick bullet-shaped head emerged just above the waves. As they approached, the otter went under. "Shy guy," Uncle Cliff said. "And there. See 'em?" He accelerated toward a red metal buoy, rocking and moaning in the waves. A tangle of long-whiskered sea lions barked as the skiff approached.

"J, you gotta see this," their father called. "There must be ten sea lions loaded on this one buoy."

Her sister remained beneath the spray skirt, her hand a fist beside her mouth, almost like she was sucking her thumb.

Uncle Cliff picked up speed again, steering them between a series of small islands, some just a single rock with a few stunted trees pushing out from the cracks. Nicky scanned the surface for cones of whale spray. Or fish jumping—any proof of that world beneath her feet.

It made her head swim, the thought that just a few inches of metal separated her from the waters, where creatures the size of their RV and bigger swam. Hundreds of them. Thousands, at this very moment. Thinking, listening, feeling, just as she did. The thought of it made her heart race. Not only the whales but also the barnacles attached to them, and the swirls of kelp lifting and falling against the rocky banks of the islands. She found herself wanting to talk to Clete about how the soil is like ocean, with all sorts of terrestrial plankton swimming through it. Such a mystery.

As the boat bounced over the waves she closed her eyes. A front of shadows, quilted into a cover of gray, overtook her. Her mind started to cartwheel as she flashed from the whales beneath her to the bleachers at a baseball game by the Susquehanna, to walking up the hill at Uncle Max's farm. She opened her eyes. With the hand that had held Josie's just minutes before, she seized the railing of the boat, trying to keep from losing her balance.

"Nicky, you okay?" her sister asked, sitting up from the cushions. "You look pale."

"I'm fine," she answered.

Uncle Cliff powered the skiff down as they approached a long dock with tires strung along the edge, attached to a ramp leading onto a tree-covered island.

"Want to make us fast?" he said to Nicky, handing her a rope and grinning expectantly. "Just wrap that line around one of those cleats."

Taking a deep breath, she gripped one of the piers to pull herself out of the boat. At the cleat she tugged the rope tight, then gave it a wrap. Josie and her dad disembarked, while Uncle Cliff came over and crouched alongside Nicky.

"That'll work, but let me show you something better," he said. "You gotta crisscross it, then tie it off."

He made a few neat wraps in an X shape, twisted the rope and flipped his wrist, and draped the oval over the cleat.

Then he looked at her. "You got a lot of gears turning in that head of yours, don't you, Nicky?"

Nicky returned a small smile. "I guess."

"I think you could maybe use a walk in the woods before salmon. I'll bet Clete would be happy to go with you, to show you some of his favorite trees."

She nodded, and followed her uncle up the uneven boards of the ramp, with Josie and their father behind. As they walked, Nicky tried to shed the vertigo that had enveloped her, sending her reeling. It felt as if something was moving inside her, something unexpected that she couldn't have predicted or prepared for.

"You get a little seasick out there?" her father said, setting a hand on her shoulder. "I sure did. I guess this place will take some getting used to. Look at this forest."

The three of them followed Cliff into the shadows of the trees. The salty ocean smell joined with a punky sweet and sour scent of sap. Josie slowed and pinched Nicky's windbreaker, pulling her back. "Did you see the look Uncle Cliff gave me when I wouldn't come out at the buoy? You know that he's the one leading the logging crew in Sky River Valley. Veronica said that he and Lars work as a team. He hates us, obviously."

"That's not true. He just stood up for us, against the mayor of the town," Nicky countered.

"He's *evil*," Josie said. "I'm not talking to him. I don't even know if I'm talking to Aunt Mall. Or Clete. I like Mom's side of the family better."

Josie's reaction didn't surprise her. She had always been quick to judge, wholeheartedly giving in to her first impressions.

But it was also nice to have her sister confiding in her like this. In a way it felt no different than walking down the block to Danville Elementary. Backpacks on, heads leaning in as they conspired. Except now they were in Alaska. Walking through a rainforest. On an island no bigger than the elementary school itself.

On top of that, Nicky knew Uncle Cliff wasn't evil. She could see it in his walk and his sparkling, bark-colored eyes. Even as he led them along the boardwalk, keeping behind Nicky in case she slipped, she could sense his gentleness. She could see he was proud of being from Shee, and she had trouble even imagining him along the sidewalks of Danville, building their father's guitar shop behind the house.

As they moved deeper into the forest a calm bloomed in her chest, smoothing over the nausea she had felt on the ride out. The trunks swayed in the wind, making creaking sounds, and the needles shirred. Moss coated rocks and spread over the earth and lower parts of the larger tree trunks. As she picked her way over the roots, she began to notice how some glistened with rain, while others had dried out to the color of bone. All around, networks of thick roots pushed out of the soil like veins. A few of the trees cupped an empty space beneath them, just like Sven's hand had demonstrated on the ferry. *Ghost trees*, she thought.

"Do bears live on these islands?" Josie asked as they walked.

"Every once in a while you'll get a swimmer," Uncle Cliff

said. "He'll sniff around for a couple days, eat a deer or two. But this island's not big enough to sustain a population. Go out Sky River Valley, or up into the mountains. That's where they live."

"Until you cut it," Josie added. "Right? Once Sky River Valley gets clearcut for the mill, then where will the bears go?"

Uncle Cliff looked back at her as they walked.

"What do you know about all that, Josie?" he asked.

"Veronica, my friend, told me that the owner, Lars Ruger, is purchasing the land from town. There's going to be a vote next Friday over whether or not he can do it. A referendum. And that you run the logging crew."

"That's right," her uncle answered. "Lars is making his case. I'm helping him. We're hoping the vote will go our way, so we can keep people on the island. Between logging and fishing, that's about all we have, now that tourism has dried up. If we don't get these trees for our saws, Jackson Cove could become a ghost town, like so many places in Southeast."

"Maybe that would be better," Josie countered. "At least it would give the land a chance to recover. The salmon could come back, and the cedars. People could just let nature alone."

"As far as I know, the cedars and the fish aren't having problems," Uncle Cliff said. "But I appreciate your interest in the situation. We'll all know more at the town hall on Wednesday."

"We will," Josie said, waving her notebook at him. "This morning in Totem Park my friend Veronica asked if I would speak out against logging. She said that people were tired of hearing her, and that a new voice would be refreshing."

"That's impressive," Uncle Cliff said, nodding his approval. "You only just got to our island, and you're speaking for it. Veronica's not from here either, though I think her mother's from Metlakatla. In any case, if you have any questions about trees, or cutting them, I'd be happy to answer. You could even visit me at the mill. I could give you a tour, which might provide some insight. I will tell you that this small town needs the money. We need land to live on. People need work at the mill to survive."

"I got all your talking points from Clete this morning," Josie said, jogging to keep pace with him. "I would also advise you, as your opponent on Wednesday, not to give me insight into your argument. Plus, what could you tell me that I can't find on the internet? Wiki has the whole history on the Tongass and Chugach, regions which I've almost memorized."

The trail started downhill. Uncle Cliff reached out a hand and ran it through bushes, coming away with a collection of red berries. He gave one to Nicky, who tasted the tart fruit, chewing thoughtfully. Josie shook her head when he offered her one.

"My people have sustained themselves on this land and these waters for a very long time, Josie. Maybe that allows me to see both sides of the issue. A lot of people want to continue to sustain themselves, living in harmony with the island. Striking the balance between taking some, and engaging with the land, and taking too much. Or too little. On

Wednesday we will hear people from both sides speak. Then on Friday, there will be a vote, and we will know where town stands. But look," he said, waving. "There's Clete, chopping cedar for us so we can have a sweet-smelling fire in the stove this evening. Fall is coming on fast. The big storms will be blowing through in no time."

Before Josie could respond, the trail opened onto a clearing with a cabin in the middle. Smoke drifted at an angle from the crooked chimney. The shingles on the cabin were weathered, worn down and splintered, caked with moss in places, reminding Nicky of her uncle's moustache. The window shutters were pinned back against the shingles with iridescent abalone shells.

Their father stopped to survey the landscape. "Cliff, you built this place? It's like a fairy tale."

"With some help," Cliff said, nodding toward Clete. "We used cutoffs from the mill, and downed trees from the island. Not too much to it. Clete and I just finished building a bridge down by the water from yellow cedar."

Clete stood surrounded by a circle of wood. Behind him was an open-sided shed with more stacked inside, each of the splits a nearly identical triangle. He landed his axe into the stump and started toward them.

"Hey!" he said. "You guys made it."

Aunt Mall came out onto the porch, holding a bowl beneath one arm and stirring with a wooden spoon. "It's the Hall family! Clete, how about you take the girls out back to pick salmonberries for the compote. The adults can have some adult beverages out on the deck."

"I don't want to pick salmonberries," Josie said, walking toward the house. "I have to practice my speech for Wednesday."

"When I have book reports I practice them by the stream," Clete said. "I make sure I can hear myself over the running water. It helps me speak louder."

"Mosquitoes would eat me," Josie said, stepping up onto the porch past Aunt Mall. "After all, aren't they the state bird of Alaska?"

"No," Clete said. "That's the willow ptarmigan. There are no mosquitoes around here. Too windy."

Josie turned to face them. "Everyone's so *literal*. Doesn't anyone make jokes?"

The screen door slammed as Josie went into the house. Aunt Mall set her mixing bowl on the porch railing. "Someone's having a rough time of it," Aunt Mall said to their father and Uncle Cliff in a low voice.

"Oh, she'll be fine," their dad said. "A little pie. A warm fire. She's just keyed up."

"You're more of an idiot than you were growing up if you think that's the truth," Aunt Mall said. "Pie isn't going to make up for losing a mother."

"That's not what I meant, Mall," her father snapped.

Aunt Mall set a hand on her brother's shoulder. "I'm sorry," she said. Then she glanced at Nicky.

"Hey, kiddo. I need you over here for a minute."

Aunt Mall led her over to where sets of boots were arranged by the porch railing. "Remember? I told you we'd get you outfitted? Salmon blood, barnacles, river rocks— your Uncle Cliff's had trees fall on his steel-toe boots and they don't hurt none. We call them Jackson Cove Slippers. Go ahead, try a pair on. Clete and you can take 'em out for a test walk."

As she slipped off her sneakers and stepped into one of the tall rubber sleeves, Nicky tried to imagine wearing them to a baseball game in Danville. Or walking along the Susquehanna. Fishing along the banks or Uncle Max's pond with her mother.

The rubber hugged her calf. The boots were the color of milk chocolate, and had a tan line around the sole. She hopped off the porch and did a turn in the mud, looking back at the zigzag of the treads. It looked as if she had left a trail of lightning bolts behind her. No, she decided; these boots were only meant for this island.

"Now, *that's* a properly outfitted Alaska girl," Aunt Mall said, grinning down at her. "Clete, why don't you show Nicky around. Here's a bowl for berries. Since getting off that ferry she looks like a pullet ready for the chicken run. Danny, you come help me cook the salmon. Cliff, you set the table."

"Break!" Uncle Cliff said.

Clete took the bowl from his mother and started toward the woods. "C'mon. We don't have a lot of time."

"Time for what?" Nicky asked, taking a few tentative steps in her new boots.

He turned back to her. "To pick salmonberries. To show you the bridge my dad and I made. And to listen to the trees, of course."

CHAPTER TWELVE

Nicky ran to catch up as Clete followed a trail of matted-down needles, bouncing from rock to rock like a mountain goat. Her new boots seemed to float over the soil. Whether it was the footwear, or the cool, clear evening, the gloom that had found her on the boat had evaporated.

"Look, those hemlocks and spruce there, growing in a line. See how their roots are raised? They all grew up from a decaying log."

"A nurse," Nicky filled in as she threaded the blankets of moss down toward a stream.

"That's right."

They reached a bright yellow bridge spanning the stream. "My dad and I built this last year," Clete said, running his palm over the glossy wood. Nicky noticed how clean her hands were compared to his. His cuticles rose like small suns along the pink of his nails. "This is yellow cedar. Tlingits use it for carvings."

"Like the tree in the valley I can see from my window. The tall one that the Three Guardsmen take care of."

"You don't forget anything, do you?" he said, looking back at her.

"It reminds me of wood my dad gets for his guitars," Nicky continued. "Is this what you were chopping?"

He shook his head. "That was red cedar. Logs float up on our beach in the big fall storms. They're left over from the log rafts, back in the eighties when people were clear-cutting for the pulp mill. Dad likes the smell, and Mom likes the colors in the stove. Blues and purples and greens from the saltwater." He stared across the water toward the mountains. "All that fluffy bright green stuff you see—those are alders, which grow in after a clearcut. This whole area was harvested—by Americans, Russians, or whoever."

He picked a few salmonberries, dropping the yellow, orange, and red clusters into his bowl. The surface of the stream reflected the white cloud cover through the trees. A fin shattered the image. Then a few more.

"Fish!" she exclaimed. Then she saw hundreds of them, pushing upriver, just beneath the surface. Strips of charcoal skin peeled off their sides, revealing chalky flesh beneath.

"Pink salmon," he remarked. "It's just a small run."

"That's what we're eating tonight?"

He laughed. "I told you, no one eats humpies except tourists. And also my grandma, sometimes. She asks me to catch the first humpy by hand, then serves it boiled with sliced onion. That's a Tlingit tradition. Pink salmon come back to the rivers after only three years—that's why they're the smallest and first to return."

She focused on the fish so he couldn't see how his laugh hurt her. "Do they come back every year?"

"Sometimes the humpies come back a year early. Those are called jack salmon. They're bright and fast, and we always try to catch them. The rest make babies and die," he said matter-of-factly.

"That's grim," she said, thinking of salmon chasing smaller fish in the ocean, growing fat before returning to this stream to lay eggs.

"Not really. It's why the trees in the rainforest are so big. They eat the fish."

"Carnivores," she said, remembering Sven on the ferry.

"Exactly. You have to be careful here. Don't ever go into the woods alone."

"Because the trees will eat you?" Nicky joked. "Now they talk, and eat, just like a bear?"

Clete inspected a berry, then ate it. "My grandmother wouldn't even let us say that word. She says they're like brothers to humans, and like to be left alone. Never look one in the eyes, that's the rule. We're all connected. And never say their name out loud. Out of respect."

A few drops of rain pinged on Nicky's hood. A shiver ran through her as she peered at the tree-covered mountains across the water.

"Sven said that if Jackson Cove wasn't careful, they'd lose their trees, and that would mean losing their fish."

"He's right," Clete said. "If town votes to cut down Sky

River Valley, the salmon won't be able to spawn in Sky River, which has the biggest run on the island. The fish need the trees as much as the trees need the fish. Instead of seeing the Old Yellow Cedar and the rest of the valley out your window, you'll see houses. Maybe even a Walmart. And fishermen like Sven will be going elsewhere to catch salmon."

"And if town votes not to sell the land to Sven's brother?"

Clete started across the bridge and up the hill. "Who knows? Maybe there won't be people left to see the view. C'mon. There's more I want to show you."

The trail curved between trees with trunks straight as the limestone columns in front of the hospital in Danville. Soft green hemlock needles brushed against her cheeks, leaving her skin moist with droplets of rainwater. Moving among the trees reminded Nicky of being in Uncle Max's cornfields just before fall harvest dried. She and Josie would run with her mother along the furrows, arms outstretched as they charged through the corridors of tawny stalks. Then they'd go to the orchards and spend hours picking Red Delicious and Granny Smiths. Her mom would have already called in to the hospital to get coverage in the ER—she always planned ahead. Setting their bushels on the kitchen counter and searching the drawers for peelers, her mom would tie on her apron, covered in wild daisies. The three of them would eat Turkey Hill with chocolate syrup before filling the kitchen with the smell of ground cloves and cinnamon and nutmeg as they made applesauce and strudel and apple butter.

She almost ran into Clete when he stopped in front of

her, staring up at a tree with long strips of gray bark. He buttoned his coat, flipped up his collar, setting his hand against the bark. Far above, needles waved in the sea breeze.

"Ready?" he said, looking at her.

"For what?" she said, not knowing what to expect. Then he closed his eyes, and leaned into the tree, as if he were trying to push it over. His nostrils flared. The pink of his nails turned to white. Then his eyes snapped open.

"I can't do it," he said.

"Do what?" Nicky asked, confused.

"I was asking the tree if I could be let in. But she's stubborn. You try."

Her eyes swept the forest. "Me? What can I do?"

"You're right," he said. "This hemlock's too dense. There's a spruce over here, who might be more welcoming." He walked over to a tree with scaly purple bark, with thick, tangled roots at the base. "This one's not so stubborn. I also think she's sleeping."

Nicky looked at Clete, then peered up into the branches, which extended like spokes from the trunk and were heaped with moss.

"This is silly," she said, reaching out to flick the bark with a fingernail. "I can hardly tell the difference between a hemlock and a spruce in the first place."

Clete nodded seriously. "Hemlock bark looks like bacon. Sitka spruce, like this one, has bark that's more like potato chips, or dragon scales. Red-purple. You might have to pinch the tree to wake her. Like this." He pulled off a shred of bark, letting it drop into the moss. "Then pretend you're a stethoscope—you know, those things doctors use to listen to your heart."

"I know what a stethoscope is," Nicky said. "My mom was a doctor."

Clete blanched. "Sorry."

"It's fine," she said, moving toward the tree. "Just tell me what to do."

He stood beside her. "First, close your eyes. Then think of pushing everything inside you, all your happiness, your hope, and your sadness into this spruce. Then see what happens."

"What *could* happen?"

"For me, it's like the bark gets gummy, and I begin to feel an electricity in my arms."

Nicky exhaled and shut her eyes. If her mother could see her doing this, surely she would laugh. *Trees can't feel, Nicky-love. That's all from your fantasy books. It makes no sense at all.*

As she planted her feet in the moss, positioning her body, she thought of her sister at the table that same morning, setting her slippers on the hardwood as she argued with Clete. Then she thought of Edward Tulane at the bottom of the sea, how he was discovered by a fisherman, who took the rabbit home with him, setting Edward on his shoulder as he walked about town. "Who dreams up these wonderful worlds?" her father would ask. Her mother would only shake her head, answering back, "Someone way out of touch with reality."

Nicky pushed her body forward, leaning her weight into the tree. Why not, for the smallest second, allow herself to believe in a world where trees could talk? Where they knew you, and even spoke of you, sending signals through their roots. . . .

At first there was nothing. Just the firmness of the bark. She found herself pushing harder, driving her feet into the earth, unwilling to give up. A flicker began in her shoulders. It grew into a tingling that spread through her hips, then swooped up the back of her neck, lighting her up from the inside.

She shut her eyes harder. The bark began to give. Before she knew what was happening, a sheet of purple rushed by in front of her, like pavement beneath a car. It felt like she had left the world behind her and was drawing deeper into a dream she knew from a long time ago. Her hair was aflame, and her chest lit up with a cool blue light as she realized she was looking *through* the spruce, at the back side of the bark. She could see veins running through it, tracks left by moisture or insects or sap—she didn't know which. Just as she was about to move, to explore this new world, she felt hands on her shoulders, pulling her back. "Nicky!"

Clete stood there in front of her, his eyes wide. She still wasn't entirely inside herself. She tried to make words. "Hey!" he said. "What happened? What did you feel?"

"I could see." She breathed. "I could see inside the tree. Things were moving. I could even see behind the bark. I mean, I was *inside*."

"Wow," Clete said. He rubbed his fingers together. "That—was incredible. We need to go to Sky River Valley. You need to see the grove, and the Three Guardsmen and

110

the Old Yellow Cedar. There are mushrooms there, they're just starting to come up."

"What about the, you know—bears?" she stammered.

"I'll bring spray," he said, starting back along the trail. "Soon—we need to go soon. Tomorrow, even."

"Sunday? That's usually our family day," Nicky said. And it was, the four of them walking into town for ice cream, or visiting Uncle Max and fishing by the pond. Nicky stealing away to walk to the top of the ridge and wander the hedgerows. All of them making pizza in the evening.

"I'm family. Tell your dad we're going for a walk. I know he doesn't want you back in the valley. But we need to do this."

"Why?" she asked.

"Because soon it's going to be dump trucks and chainsaws and excavators!" he cried. "Don't you see? Lars Ruger has been going around town making all sorts of promises. If this vote doesn't pass, he says his mill will close. The supply stream of old growth from Prince of Wales Island is drying up. My father says if we're cutting, it has to be in the fall. They don't want to waste time."

"Why is everything happening so quickly?"

"Because people need the jobs. And they need to cut before the fall storms, and also before the sap starts running in the trees. That way the logs will keep longer in the lumberyard and will be easier to mill."

"We just got here," Nicky said. "Like, yesterday."

"You got here at a crazy time," Clete said as he crossed the bridge, picking up the bowl of salmonberries from the railing. "Before the virus, no one thought this could actually happen. Now my dad says it *needs* to happen if Jackson Cove is going to survive."

"Just—stop for a second," Nicky said, running along the boards to catch up with him. "I'll go," she said, "into the valley. But first you need to stop pretending that the trees need me, or have some message I need to hear that will make some big difference."

"Nicky, what just happened there?" Clete asked.

She thought about it, and couldn't answer.

"It's taken me years to get that far. It took you, like, ten seconds." He tapped his boot against the moss. "If town votes to keep the land, then Lars will shut the mill. That's a fact. If that happens, then my dad says we'll need to move to Oregon, where he can get work either on a logging crew or in a mill. Mom would have to leave her job at the newspaper. We'll need to sell our place on the island, probably to some rich folks in Seattle, and this home that my dad and I built will be lost. That's what's happening here, and not just to my parents. It's eighty percent of the people here who depend on the mill in one way or another."

Nicky thought of the sweet little handmade cabin she had glimpsed from the top of the hill. She couldn't imagine anyone else living in it. She had only just arrived—now her cousin might disappear?

"So—which would you rather have happen? The mill shut down, or lose the valley?" she asked him.

"I told you," Clete said. "I kind of agree with your sister. Those trees are my best friends. I'd rather leave the Old

Yellow Cedar, the Guardsmen, and the rest of them than see that valley get cut."

Nicky stood there, trying to imagine that space between the two mountainsides slashed clear, just a thatch of limbed branches.

"Nicky, listen to me," Clete said slowly. "I'm done trying to convince you. Tomorrow morning I'm going to skiff in, and we're going to walk up to Sky River Valley. Then you'll see for yourself why the trees need you, and stop asking so many questions. No one else knows this, but believe me, it's true."

Nicky looked back at him. "Sorry. It's just a lot."

"I know," he said as he turned back toward the cabin and started up the hill. "We're just running out of time. Tomorrow you'll see what I'm talking about."

CHAPTER THIRTEEN

That evening, after eating smoked, grilled, and baked salmon, along with Aunt Mall's yummy salmonberry dessert, Uncle Cliff skiffed them back to town. The girls brushed their teeth and climbed into bed, Josie complaining about the smell of fresh paint, but falling right asleep.

Nicky turned over in her bed and parted the curtains. She set her chin in her hands and scanned Sky River Valley.

The trees made an evergreen blanket between the slopes of the mountains; a shadow line appeared where Sky River ran through. Nicky rested her forehead against the cold glass, watching the pointed tips of the spruce and hemlocks sway in the breeze. She could still feel in her palms how the bark stopped resisting her, how the ridges had melted beneath her skin. The bolt of blue had left her feeling cleared out, quiet, and hopeful, such a contrast to the dizziness she felt on the skiff. But the idea of meeting the Three Guardsmen tomorrow, and the Old Yellow Cedar, frightened her.

They were only trees, yet when Sven and Clete talked about them, they seemed alive, almost like people.

It was coming up on nine o'clock, and the sun was setting over the canopies. Unlike the fields of corn in Pennsylvania, which moved in waves in the golden sunshine, as if some dragon blew hot breath across the stalks, these trees seemed to wobble to their own particular beat. Some made gentle ellipses, while others remained still. Nicky wondered if this was because of how the branches fit into one another, or how the roots folded together, like some melody. The sensation of energy when she slipped inside the spruce almost felt like music, the spell of her father's brass slide moving over the steel strings.

She turned over, pulled the covers to her chin, and imagined herself as a bright green sapling pushing out of the dark soil. Her two arms shot out smooth branches as her trunk rose into the air. Bark spread over her legs, ridges appearing as they fused into a single taproot. A salmon finned at the base of her trunk, a deer paused to smell the tips of her needles. Far in the distance, a bear lumbered along the banks of the river, leaving impressions in the moss as he moved toward her. All around she could feel a gentle popping in the soil, thousands of twitches moving up from the roots into her core.

Trees have no central nervous system. How could they communicate? Unlike in Pennsylvania, where trees grew in patches left between fields, the spruce and hemlocks and cedar of this valley made one dark green blanket. How could *they* not be connected beneath the soil? And if they were connected, how could they not be communicating, working together like a family, like one big nervous system?

Of course the mother trees would recognize their young, taking care of the saplings, sending nutrients through the network Clete told her about to make sure their children grew up safe and healthy. All of it happening beneath the soil, which—like Clete said—was really no different from the ocean: a sprawling dark space that humans didn't really understand. Where things happened so slowly that humans hardly noticed. *Just because we don't understand doesn't mean it's not happening,* Nicky thought.

Nicky looked down at the covers, thinking of her own heart on the right side of her chest, pushing blood to her hands and feet and head. The swirl of liquid keeping her body moving and alert. How could she, this one single person, be expected to help this valley? To absorb all its sadness and strangeness while keeping her own her brain awake to the world, especially after losing her own mother? She scrunched her toes together, the muscles in the balls of her feet aching from pushing into the soil earlier that evening. She flipped up her hood, folded her arms over her chest, and gazed up at the attic rafters.

It wasn't fair. The world was asking too much of her.

Nicky knew if she told Josie about what had happened with the spruce, her twin would laugh. "Some people pick cats or dogs or invisible friends to talk to. But you, Nicky— you talk to trees. When you're old, you'll have like forty trees around you instead of cats."

"I hope so," Nicky would respond. "It's called living in a forest."

No matter how they both evolved, Nicky felt sure that she'd always be in Josie's life. She had always known, by the way their mother had reacted to each of them, that they moved through the world differently. Josie seemed much more at ease in her mother's world of explanation—this happened because of this, and so forth. A world that left no room for imagination.

Now that their mother was gone, Josie's decision to dye her hair, or become a vegetarian, or devote herself to yoga, or even drink coffee, struck Nicky as calculated rebellions she knew her father would reject. Her insistence on counting the days—the seconds, even—until she was eighteen, when she could be "free," annoyed Nicky more than it annoyed her father. Why couldn't she just appreciate the time the three of them had together?

Their mother had been deeply caring, a listener, always finding points in common with her patients, or anyone, really. Over the past few weeks, Nicky had watched Josie react in ways that made it clear she had no interest in what others were thinking or feeling. She just bent up her face, gave some rude response, and moved on.

As children, their mom had warned them against this, saying that one day their grumpy faces might freeze and become permanent. Nicky knew twins started out symmetrical, and over the years begin to reflect their sadness and happiness separately. She expected that her face would begin to show watchfulness, sadness, and even disappointment, while her sister's would harden into a look of defiance. Her brow sloping, her eyes growing smaller. Josie the bulldog. Nicky the basset hound.

She closed her eyes. It was nice having a cousin on the island who was also quiet, and a little shy. She could see that Clete respected her, even treating her like some sort of wizard. Someone with powers to hear what others could not. To heal what others couldn't.

Maybe I do have a special power, she thought. No. Josie the supersmart one, Josie the go-getter. When there was a problem, Josie always found a way out. Adults didn't intimidate her. They were just another challenge to overcome.

Except here in Alaska, things seemed different. People seemed to respond to Nicky's quietness and flinch at her sister's brazen nature. She couldn't quite put her finger on it, but this island felt like *her* place, even if she still wasn't convinced that the trees had been expecting her.

Despite her fear of bears, and of the Three Guardsmen and Old Yellow Cedar, she found herself eager to wake up and walk with Clete into this valley so neatly framed by the glass of her window. She was beginning to *trust* the island, that it would take care of her and not let anything bad happen. Uncle Cliff, Aunt Mall, even Sven, seemed to glow with a sort of possibility, and goodness, and promise. Nicky had never felt that people other than her family truly cared for her. Here on the island, just by virtue of living on the Rock, as Veronica called it in her video, she seemed to earn the trust and admiration of others, maybe because she had chosen—or her father had chosen, more accurately—to come to the state and make it home.

Nicky squeezed her eyes shut, pulling the covers tight over her. Out in the dark, a raven chortled, getting comfortable in the branches for the evening. After a moment she rolled over again and scooted forward in the covers, gripping the sash of the window and lifting it open all the way. A gust of lemon-scented air blew in, spiced with something else—yellow cedar, she guessed. The oldest trees in the forest. The wet boardwalk below reflected the amber streetlight. The moon emptied its light over the valley, shading the treetops gray.

As she leaned forward through the open window, staring at the expanse of the valley beneath her, the trees themselves turned to bark, each one a scale attached to the trunk stretching the length of the valley. The crown lay invisible, somewhere beyond the mountains, stretching its branches to the edges of the island, while the roots curled under the streets of town. The roots reaching far beneath the boardwalk and cement to the ocean, where salmon charged about in the dark, searching for needlefish, waiting for a signal to return to the forest that bore them. To the trees that protected them from predators and saved them from floods. Trees that, each year, took back their spent bodies, which melted back into the banks of the river from whence they came.

PART THREE

Going Into
Sky River Valley

CHAPTER FOURTEEN

Sunday morning, when she came downstairs, Nicky found Josie at the kitchen table, slicing grapes into her oatmeal. Watermelon stretched out on the back of her neck, gulping down a blueberry. The iguana twitched as Nicky sat down and picked a couple grapes from the bowl.

"Hey. Get your own."

Nicky ignored Josie as she chewed, looking out the window at the low gray clouds. "Happy Sunday to you too. Is Dad still sleeping?"

"Either that, or someone let a bear in the house. What's up with the cargo pants and raincoat?" Josie asked. "You look like you're going on an expedition."

"Clete wanted to show me a few things around town."

"Oh," Josie mumbled, squeezing honey over her oatmeal. "I guess I'm not invited."

"You want to come?" Nicky said, excited that her sister might join them, but also appreciating the opportunity to get revenge on her sister for saying she couldn't come to Totem Park with Veronica.

"I'm practicing for my speech on Wednesday. Dad's helping me," Josie said, swallowing a grape.

"I can't believe you're going to be talking."

"Someone needs to explain to people here that it takes a five-hundred-year-old tree five hundred years to grow back. Might as well be me."

Nicky heard a knock at the bottom of the stairs. She grabbed a few more grapes and started for the door.

"Hey, Nick," Josie said.

"What?" Nicky said, turning.

Josie paused, then carefully set down her spoon full of oatmeal, as if considering her question. Her eyes flashed.

"How often do you think of her?"

It took Nicky a moment to understand the question. Then she realized that she hadn't thought of her mother once the entire morning. A feeling of guilt washed over her. "Four. Maybe five times a day. Sometimes I talk to her, even though she's not there. Just to tell her I'm okay, or that Dad misses her. Or that you miss her," she added. "Sometimes I just say I love you, and I wish you were here."

"Do you ever get mad at her?" Josie whispered.

"No. Not really," Nicky said. "Do you?"

Josie picked up the knife she had used to cut the grapes, examining it for nicks. Watermelon's throat shifted as he swallowed the blueberry.

"I see her all the time. When I do, I usually just say hi. Then she goes away, and I get angry all over again. I hate it."

Nicky started across the room, wanting to hug her sister. Josie cut her off, standing and taking her bowl to the sink. "Have fun with Clete," she said. "Go talk to the trees, or commune with nature, whatever you do."

"I love you," Nicky stammered.

"Okay," Josie said, moving past her to go to the attic.

At the bottom of the stairs, Nicky took her windbreaker from the hook and pulled the door open. Clete stood in the light rain, his hands in the pockets of his camouflage coat.

"Hey," she said. "Sorry it took me so long."

"It's okay. You have gloves?" he asked.

"No. My hands won't be cold."

"It's not for the cold. It's for thorns. I have an extra pair. Ready?"

She zipped her windbreaker and stepped outside. She heard the scrape of a window, and looked up to see her father leaning out. "Hey, Clete," he called out.

"Hi, Uncle Danny," Clete said, squinting into the rain.

"Where you guys off to?"

"A walk," Nicky answered.

"Have a good time." He waved, and Nicky gave him a quick wave back as they started down the gravel road.

"Did you bring the spray?" Nicky asked.

Clete held up a red bottle that resembled a small fire extinguisher. "Their bellies are full of fish. That means they're not aggressive. They'll hear us way before we see them."

"I'd rather not take chances."

Clete gave her a mischievous smile. "I thought you wanted to see one."

At the bottom of the road, he turned left instead of right. They walked in silence along the sidewalk by the harbor. A car passed, its windshield wipers making a squeaking sound.

"Next time I come into town, I'll bring a bike for you," Clete said. "So you can get around quicker."

"Thanks," Nicky said.

At the old boarding school campus they turned left again, following a path that led into a grassy quadrangle bordered by brown-shingled buildings.

"My grandmother on my Dad's side went to school here," Clete said, pointing at one of the structures. Its brown paint was peeling, and one of the doors hung off its hinges. "She lived in that building over there. It was a Presbyterian school."

"My grandfather—well, your grandfather too—was a Presbyterian minister," Nicky responded. "In Danville. We lived across from his church in an old house with stained-glass windows."

Clete nodded. "My mom told me about it. That's where she grew up."

"Mom and Dad did a really good job making the house pretty again."

"That's cool," Clete said as they passed a broken window in one of the buildings. "My grandmother hated this school. She said if you were caught speaking Tlingit you'd get hit with a ruler on the back of the neck."

"My mother said the same thing happened to her, except on the knuckles, at Catholic school."

"Where did she grow up?"

"In a small coal-mining town called Ashland. Her dad was a miner who came from Italy. I never met him."

"My dad says the forest is his church," Clete said. "When he hunts, he says he finds God."

"That's strange," Nicky said, enjoying the light rain on her cheeks and the growing heat in her muscles as they crested the hill. "And he still wants to cut down Sky River Valley?"

"He says that just like the salmon and the deer give themselves, so the trees provide in times of need. He tells me that the trees want us to be here, where my father's family has been for so long. White people are so obsessed with wilderness and untouched nature. That's just not how we think about the forest."

"Do you agree?" Nicky asked. "About cutting down the valley?"

"No," Clete said. "I think it's different. The scale is different. Yes, you take five berries and leave one. If you take that valley, you're wiping out an entire family. For example, I'd never shoot a doe with fawns. Neither would my dad," he added.

They cut through a patch of woods and came out on a wide asphalt road. Cars rushed past. At a break in traffic they crossed, passing the Alaska State Trooper Academy. Cobalt blue cars with black matte hoods dark with rain were parked in front. Clete gestured toward the building. "That's where my dad says I'm going when I turn eighteen. To be an Alaska state trooper."

"But you don't want to?" Nicky asked.

He shook his head. "That's the problem. I love working with wood, but I hate killing trees."

"Sounds like a problem," Nicky agreed.

The woods grew thicker as they left the main street and followed the packed gravel of Sky River Road. The rush of cars receded. A few houses appeared through the trees. Nicky heard the gurgle of a river off to the right. Along the side of the road she saw a medicine cabinet with a cracked mirror stuck in the brush. She went over and tapped the rusting metal box with the toe of her boot. It made a tinny, echoing sound. She leaned over and opened the door. Inside she saw a series of circles rusted into the enamel shelves, where bottles had once rested.

She closed the door again, then peered at her reflection in the mirror, noting how determined she looked in the tarnished glass. She pushed the hood of her windbreaker off her head and held her gaze, not minding the rain in her hair.

Clete joined her in the mirror. The two of them stood there, watching their reflections. The intensity of her eyes reminded her of her mother before she left for work. Maybe these were Josie's eyes, but not hers.

"Now that everyone thinks that Lars Ruger is going to cut the valley, they're leaving their junk back here," Clete commented.

Fog rolled in behind them, covering the tree trunks. With an effort Nicky broke the stare.

"What about your mom?" she asked his reflection. "Does she ever come into the woods?"

"No," Clete said back at her. She saw fog behind them in the mirror, winding between the tree trunks.

With an effort Nicky broke the stare. As they continued down the road, Clete said, "Trees scare her. She said that when she was growing up in Pennsylvania, her parents told her that monsters lived in the woods, and she never got over it. The only way she'd agree to live here is on a small island so she wouldn't have to worry."

"That's funny," Nicky said. "She doesn't seem like someone who gets scared."

The fog continued to thicken. From high above she heard the squeak of a bald eagle. The asphalt ended. A tangle of bushes grew at the base of the trailhead, where a drab wooden sign said SKY RIVER VALLEY TRAIL—5.6 MILES. Below that, another read BE AWARE OF BEAR. There was a bear print, four ovals and four points making a shape that resembled a campfire.

"You ready?" Clete said. "Our cutoff for the grove is only about two miles in. After the first bridge."

Now that they were here, standing at the trailhead, she was having second thoughts. She'd never be able to find her way back to town if something happened to Clete. No one on the island knew where they were going or what they were doing.

"Do these trees, the Old Yellow Cedar and the Three Guardsmen, whatever they're called, know we're coming?"

Clete only laughed. "You still don't believe me about any of this, do you?"

"If I didn't trust you, I wouldn't be here. It's the part about them having a message for me I'm not sure about."

Clete turned to her, took a moment to redo the bun in his hair, then hitched his thumbs in the pockets of his coat. The ease with which he stood, his arms bent at the elbows, and his shoulders square, reminded Nicky of her mother.

"I know it's difficult to imagine, but all these trees here, they're alert. Their reactions are slower—a third of an inch per second, to be exact. It's like having a slower heartbeat, but they're just as alive as we are. All the things that we experience—friendship, love, pain, and hunger—trees feel too. I'm not making it up. It's been proven," he insisted. His eyes shone above his damp cheeks.

"Maybe," Nicky said, wanting to believe him in the same way she always believed her mother. "Maybe trees experience these things individually. But their roots don't, you know, grab each other. They're not joined."

"Trees can become friends, and their roots can intermingle. They can share sunlight. When one dies, the other usually dies right after it. But you're right. They don't attach at the roots. Mushrooms do it for them, building these networks beneath the soil, like electrical lines. Then the trees send messages on the wires. It's like the internet, except in the soil."

"The Wood Wide Web," Nicky filled in.

"Right. It's not only messages they send, but also food. Mom trees feed their babies sugar. Other trees poison each other, like the Three Guardsmen, or black walnuts, to keep saplings from growing too close. But most trees cooperate. That is the part my father doesn't understand. They're a family. When one goes down, they all start to fall apart. The rest of the forest doesn't survive."

Nicky realized she had been holding her breath. She exhaled, gazing into the trees in front of her.

"C'mon," he said, stepping past the wooden sign onto the trail. "We're losing time."

As they walked Nicky found herself examining where the tree trunks pushed out from the moss-covered soil. Just as the whale she had seen on the ferry took her down into the depths of an ocean she had never really considered, Clete's words, and these towering hemlock and spruce trees she now walked beneath, plunged her imagination into the soil below. She could see in front of her filaments sent out by mushrooms, thick roots, stones, even underground rivers, all of it holding these trees together.

The trees in Sky River Valley grew even taller, maybe twice as tall as the trees near town. Far, far above she could only make out fragments of sky among their arching crowns.

Ahead, Clete climbed a stairway of river rocks and roots glistening with rainwater. The soles of her boots seemed to mold to the contours of the trail as she came along behind him.

"Have you heard the story of the Lady of the volcano?" Clete asked. Nicky shook her head.

"It was one my grandmother's brother told me. His name was S'áaxwshaan, which means 'Old Hat.' He said that when the Tlingits returned to the land after the last ice age, there was only grass and alders on the land, but no evergreens. When they came to this land, they saw smoke from the volcano, and the mountain was blinking and spouting fire. But the men in the canoes still found trees nearby where the lava hadn't reached.

"Then a woman appeared to them. She was dressed in white deerskins, which are deerskins left out to be bleached in the winter sun, that's what he said. The woman in white said the island should be left alone. The Tlingit medicine man stepped up, all dressed for trouble—that's how S'áaxwshaan described it when he told me the story. But then the woman in white noticed the beautiful earrings and bracelets the Tlingit women wore, and she took them for gifts in return for letting the Tlingit return to the island.

"They built first on the island with the volcano, and then here on Shee. At'iká is Tlingit for 'on the outside of,' and the people from the inside waters started calling settlers here Sheet'iká Kwáan, which means 'people on the outside edge of Shee Island.' My grandmother always told me never to forget how slow time passes, and how we are all part of something much larger than any of our small bodies, which spend such a short time on this earth. We can't truly understand trees, she always said, because we see so little of their lifespan."

The more Clete spoke, the more Nicky felt like she was stepping into a story she had once known and loved, but had forgotten. The same with the land—she recognized the volcano, and these trees. As she walked she thought that she could even be content living the rest of her life in the cool light of this forest, without ever seeing another piece of plastic or a computer or cellphone again. The heady smell of sap and the power of Clete's story filled her with both strength and awe in the same way the Presbyterian church back in Danville once had, with its vaulted ceilings and purple stained-glass windows.

When Clete stopped ahead of her, she was so deep in her thoughts, imagining the woman in white putting on her jewelry, that she almost ran into him. He poked a pile of green mush with a stick.

"You have any songs you like to sing?" he asked. "Because it sure looks to me like that is some fresh poop."

Her heart revved in her chest. The feeling of peace and wonder evaporated. The pile was as big as a funnel cake.

"That looks really big," she said.

"Big poop, big animal. That's also what S'áaxwshaan would say."

A soft wind moved through the bramble. Above her a branch creaked.

"*The bear went over the volcano . . . ,*" Nicky started. She caught herself as Clete laughed.

"Sorry. How about 'Row Row Row Your Boat'?" He nodded and joined in, the two of them bellowing out the song as they walked.

The trail swung back to the river. When they reached the water Clete led the way up a series of yellow stumps arranged into steps. They crossed to the halfway point of the cedar, the log flexing beneath their weight. Clete stopped and poured tea from his thermos, holding a steaming cup out to her. The hot liquid warmed her chest.

Clete sipped and stared into the current. Nicky thought he was going to tell her another story. Instead, he said, "It's kinda silly, isn't it, having children, then swimming off to die." As he spoke, what she had thought were rocks below transformed into hundreds of salmon.

Clete's eyes slid toward her. "Sorry," he mumbled.

"Why?" Nicky said, focused on the fish below.

"I mean, with your mother." His eyes shined. "That wasn't nice. Also, what I said earlier. You know, about trees dying, and families falling apart."

Nicky considered this as she watched the river run beneath the bridge. "Listen. I know my mother's dead. We all do. It's no secret. So you don't have to tiptoe around it."

He continued to watch her, as if he didn't believe her words. "I wish I had known her, my aunt," he said. "Mom says she was really smart. Like, *really* smart. Maybe not friendly. But when she smiled, it was like the sun fell on you. That's what she said."

Nicky didn't know how to respond. After a moment, Clete screwed the thermos cap back on. "Just a little farther," he said, starting again across the log bridge.

The trail arced away from the river, and the forest grew quiet again as they left the chatter of the riffles behind them. Heavy drops thudded into the moss. Nicky kept running Clete's words over in her head. It was true. When her mother smiled, like when she saw Josie and Nicky running up the driveway toward her at the end of the day and smiled through the truck windshield, there was nothing better. A smile both exciting and reassuring. That everything was going to be okay.

Ahead, Clete paused.

"This is it, where the game trail breaks off. Ready?" He handed her a pair of thick gloves. "My mom uses these for cutting back brush. They're also good for devil's club."

Without waiting for a response, he disappeared into the wall of green.

"Clete?" Nicky said.

"I'm here," a voice said. "Just duck your head. Don't touch the bottom of the leaves, there are thorns there too."

The heart-shaped leaves shook back and forth in the breeze, as if taunting her. *This is so stupid,* she thought. *Thorns and talking trees and grizzly bears.* On top of that, she had never lied to her father. If he found out, he'd never treat her the same again. Trust was a big deal for him. Josie was one thing—she had always gone her own way, dying her hair in the sink at the RV park, or whatever. But Nicky was never dishonest. She knew he depended on her. Even more now.

The wind coursed through the branches, pushing at her back. She thought of the view from her window, the Old Yellow Cedar standing high above the other trees. Then of the medicine man dressed for trouble, and the woman in white deerskins. She looked down at her gloves and took a deep breath. With her elbows protecting her face, Nicky flung herself forward, gritting her teeth against the thorns as they tore at her wrists. She closed her eyes, trying to push aside the pain. Her boots squelched into the mud. The leaves parted, and Clete stood there waiting.

"Okay?" he said, starting forward.

"Okay," she confirmed.

They crossed a small stream running through the moss,

and climbed to an open expanse of grass pocked with small brown puddles. Miniature trees draped with aqua-colored lichen grew up from the soil, which flexed with each of their steps.

"This is a muskeg," Clete told her as he pulled a few strands of lichen from the branches and put them into his pocket. "This is called Old Man's Beard. Always good to have for fire-starter. That, and sap from Sitka spruce."

Ahead of her she heard a branch snap, and she froze, sure that a bear was going to lunge from the leaves. Clete's head turned to the fringe of the muskeg just as a brown shape rose from the brush, charging away from them.

Clete exhaled, smiling back. "Blacktail. We startled him."

"Would your dad have shot?" she asked, trying to calm her thudding heart.

"Probably," Clete said. "In August you can only take bucks. He was a forky, a smaller one."

They climbed a hill of trees separating the lower muskeg from the higher one, which was longer and wider. Networks of black mud trails pocked with deer hoof tracks wove through the grass. The sun emerged, lighting up the gnarled trees growing from the swamp, which Clete called dwarf pines. Her XtraTufs sunk into the spongy soil. It moved ahead of her like a wave. Water bugs skated along the surface of the silty brown puddles.

"Almost there," Clete called out.

Even as she saw the thick block of trees ahead of her, it was difficult to imagine how some of the world's tallest, oldest trees could emerge from this forest. The dwarf pines, which Clete said could be hundreds of years old, were short and twisted. She caught up to where he waited, at the edge of the muskeg. He had removed his can of bear spray from its holster.

"We need to hurry if we're going to make it back by dinner. Luckily the sun's breaking out, but that could just be a sucker hole."

"What's a sucker hole?" she asked.

He smiled. "For suckers who think it's about to get sunny."

"Oh."

"Ready?" he asked.

She didn't move. Her legs wouldn't budge.

"Nicky," Clete said slowly. "Are you okay?"

She nodded. "Actually being out here—it's just a lot of feeling."

"I understand. It's just—if town votes to cut these trees, we might never see any of this again. Not the muskeg, or the dwarf pines. This might be our last chance. Okay?"

"Okay."

Then he disappeared into the bushes.

She shut her eyes and took a deep breath. She brought her elbows to her face, and pushed through.

CHAPTER FIFTEEN

When she opened her eyes again, she saw in front of her hundreds of the tallest, straightest, most beautiful trees she could have ever imagined. Clusters of ferns grew around their bases, the fronds dotted with raindrops. Mist shifted through the branches, furred with moss, making wreaths around the bark. Below, lush hills of moss rose and fell like waves between the behemoths.

Clete pointed toward a group of gray-trunked trees, growing upward like long waterfalls tumbling from the sky. "The Guardsmen," he whispered.

A drop of rain fell on the back of her hand, sending the smallest of currents through her palm, up her wrist. She pushed a few curls, damp from the drizzle, behind her ears.

"They must be taller than skyscrapers," she said. "I can't even see the tops."

"Shhh," Clete said.

Nicky stood still, letting the kaleidoscope of trees resolve in front of her. One by one the trunks separated, as if introducing themselves. They took on individual characteristics—a crooked branch here, moss draped like a pair of pants drying over there. The trees grew on such a different scale from the black walnut, or even the Norway spruces, on Uncle Max's farm.

Behind the Three Guardsmen, a wall of brown rose. Then her eyes put together the puzzle of moss-heavy branches, attaching them to the same trunk. It was one entire tree, she realized, thick as a rowhome in downtown Danville.

"That's the Old Yellow Cedar," Clete said. "Older than America. Probably older than the Renaissance."

The needles were the color of the ocean, and sprayed out in feathery plumes. "It's—amazing," Nicky said.

"It will be one of the first trees to go, because it's so valuable."

Her ears picked out not only the rush of the creek, and the uneven warbling of a bird, but a faint hum rising from the soil. That green pieces of paper, or numbers on a computer screen, could be exchanged for these living pillars pushing up from the lush moss baffled her.

She lifted her chin, focusing on a raven hopping along a thick trunk that had fallen over the river. Water rushed beneath. She smelled something rich and sweet, similar to the mulch her mother poured into their window boxes in Danville. The smell of death and life blended together, the beginning and end captured in a single scent.

"Ready?" Clete said.

"For what?"

"To cross."

Before she could respond he scrambled up the fallen log. The raven hopped in the other direction as Clete started toward the grove. Her head told her to stay put. She didn't need to be part of this adventure. Her heart hammered in her chest.

Then her feet were moving through the moss, and she was setting her toes against knots in the tree. She climbed to the top, the river far beneath her.

It was too late to turn back. She had to meet these trees.

Chapter Sixteen

C lete was ahead of her, already in the middle of the log, setting one boot in front of the other. Nicky fought back her fear, trying not to look down at the stream rushing beneath her. *When you're scared, take small steps*, her mother had told her. *Make no sudden moves.*

She stretched her arms out to either side for balance, took a couple steps, then a few more. This wasn't hard. One foot in front of the other. She was almost to the middle of the log when she saw, along the stream bank, prints, an exact match of those on the wooden board at the trailhead. A bear claw, big as an oven mitt. Beside them a set of smaller tracks hugged the stream bank. Her heart lurched. A bear and her cub.

Nicky didn't want to yell out to Clete, for fear of causing him to lose his balance. She also didn't want to say the word *bear*. But the thought of being eaten made it difficult to move. Stuck in the middle of the log, she peered back down to where the riffles bunched up in front of the rocks. Clouds blocked the sun, and the land fell into shadow. Darker now, the stream looked deeper and faster and farther below than it had from the edge. The five holes in the print, where the claws punched the sand, seemed bottomless.

"Nicky!" She heard Clete calling from the other side. He beckoned her with a hand. "Don't stop walking."

She pushed her fear down and found the courage to take another step. The sun reemerged, the moss turned bright again, and the contours on the log beneath her sharpened. With a leap she came down, tumbling into the soft ferns.

"Get your spray out! I saw a print in the sand," she said as she pulled herself up from the wetness.

He smiled at her. "That's old," he said. "The edges are windblown, not crisp."

His easy tone reassured her. He knew this forest, and it wasn't like she'd ever be out here alone.

She followed him to the base of one of the giant hemlocks, allowing her heart to calm. Nicky ran her palms over the tree, feeling the bumps, the crumble against her skin as the bark flaked off. A pulse went through her, and she snatched her hand back.

"What was that?" Clete asked, inspecting her. "Did you feel something?"

She stepped beyond the hemlock and approached the gnarled cedar, with its paper-thin layers of shedding bark. At the base of the trunk, mushrooms pushed up in clusters from the moss, their caps shiny with moisture. She kept her hands folded to her chest as she walked.

"Probably the oldest tree in the valley," Clete said, looking up into the branches. "Sometimes I think it's my best friend on the island. Usually the mushrooms aren't out this early."

She crouched beside one. The middle of the cap appeared toasted, the top folded down along the rim, giving way to ridges beneath.

"Close your eyes. Try not to think of anything," he told her.

Dampness from the soil spread across her knee. She reached her finger beneath one of the mushroom caps. Immediately a buzzing began in her head, a single unbroken line of sound, sharp and insistent. She snatched her hand back. The sound faded.

Breathing deeply, she reached out again, this time gripping the mushroom, even as the buzzing filled her ears. She tried not to panic, keeping her hand in place as the current returned to her arm. It unfurled along her shoulders, up her neck, shaking out along the back of her head, lighting up the roots of her hair. She swallowed. The back of her throat began to feel dry and sore. It was hard to get a breath, and her molars were starting to ache, the sour metal taste when you bite into aluminum foil.

With an effort she broke free of the mushroom. As if someone flipped off a switch, the buzzing stopped. Clete watched her, his hands out in front, ready to catch her.

"What was *that?*" she asked. It had been stronger than with the spruce on Clete's island, though not as disorienting. Her whole body seemed to twitch and fizz. She stared up into the branches of the great cedar, whose crown vanished into the milky white clouds. *This tree is testing me*, she thought. *It wants to see if I'm scared.*

"Nicky, maybe this is too much," Clete said, scanning the forest. "You look pale. I don't want to be out here if something happens. Let's go home—we can come back next weekend."

"You just said next weekend is too late," Nicky said as she rolled the sleeve of her windbreaker, then curled her palm around the stalk of the largest mushroom.

Instantly a screeching started in her ears. Her chest seized. A new wave of energy passed through her. Then came another, and another, and soon she heard a chorus of screams, both joyful and scared, one layered over the other. She knew in an instant that she would never be able to unclench her hand by herself. The current held her in place. She blinked a few times, turning toward Clete. He was saying something, but she couldn't make it out. Something else filled her ears. Not words, or anything close to them. But a moist, insistent sound, a warble that evened into a keening, steady and clean and urgent.

Damp hair fell over her eyes. As the sound echoed through her, she fell deeper, deeper into a cavern, with no way to get out. She looked down at the mushroom, searching its brown cap for an answer. Then up at the moss-heavy branches of the cedar. Just before she felt herself about to lose consciousness, the screeching in her ears quieted, and she was still. *You came*, the trees said.

She felt Clete's hands grip her shoulders, pulling at her. The mushroom exploded from the ground, and she stumbled back into the moss. This time, flashes continued to go off in her head, even as the buzzing faded. Slowly, like a storm passing, her mind cleared.

"This is too much," Clete said. "We need to go back. These trees, it's too much for one person."

She arched her neck to stare up at the Old Yellow Cedar, then across at the Three Guardsmen.

"They're crying," she whispered. "The trees. They're crying, and also laughing. It makes no sense."

Moss hanging from the lower branches of the cedar swayed in the wind.

"Did they say anything?" Clete asked.

Nicky searched her mind. She could almost taste the words the trees had given her. They circled along the roof of her mouth, then seemed to settle, clear and bright in front of her. Just like Clete had said—too much for one person.

"They said they want me to save them."

CHAPTER SEVENTEEN

When she opened the door to their apartment, her father's guitar stopped.

"Nicky?!"

He appeared at the top of the stairs, then ran down and took her by the shoulders. "Where have you been? I was about to call the troopers. I just got back from the mill and couldn't find you anywhere."

"Clete and I were on the boat, just fishing for . . ." She tried to remember the word Clete had told her, by way of excuse. "Duskies. In the channel," she added.

She sat on the bench and started pulling off her boots, trying to act calm. Her father's eyes appeared large and watery behind his glasses. He wore khakis and a button-down shirt.

"Why are you dressed up?" she asked.

"I was out visiting Uncle Cliff at the mill."

"On a Sunday?"

He paused. "He wanted to show me the floor when things were quiet. That's a long time to go fishing," he said.

"The day turned nice, and we stopped on an island and walked in the tide pools. I was having such a good time."

"Well, that makes me happy," he said, his voice relieved. "C'mon up. It's Sunday pizza night. Your sister and I have been cutting up toppings. And next time, if you're going to be out for so long, tell me. I know you don't like phones, but fall's coming, and the days are getting shorter, and I don't want you out alone in the dark."

"Sorry, Dad," Nicky said, hugging him.

They started up the stairs. At the top Josie stood waiting. She grabbed Nicky's arm as their father passed into the kitchen.

"Let go! What's your problem?" Nicky asked.

"Where were you?"

"With Clete. On the skiff."

"You're lying," Josie hissed. "I saw Clete's boat tied up at the harbor."

Nicky heard the clink of her father stacking plates in the dish rack. He hummed whatever blues song he had been playing, then started to sing. *"If I ever get back on the killing floor..."*

Nicky unpeeled Josie's fingers from her arm. "We were in the woods, okay? Did you practice your speech?"

"Yes," Josie said quickly. The ceiling light was behind her, making her eyes difficult to read. "Don't ever lie to me," Josie said flatly. "We're twins. No secrets."

"Don't start telling me about secrets," Nicky said. "You've been keeping secrets since we left Danville."

"What are you talking about?"

Nicky pulled back. "I'm talking about you don't talk to me anymore. Or to Dad. You don't share stuff. You remember when we caught fireflies together on Uncle Max's farm? Or getting ice cream, or you and Mom yelling at baseball games? Or both of us in our tree, waiting for her to come home?"

Josie stood silhouetted before her. Her green hair appeared black. Her brow furrowed.

"I'm sorry for lying," Nicky said. "But I want my best friend back. I want my old sister back."

Josie's features softened, and her shoulders went slack. Nicky reached out, thinking that her sister might faint. As she did, Josie's features hardened, and she stood up tall. "You're deflecting. It's a beginner's debate tactic. Bringing emotions into the fight. I'm not going to fall for it. It's not a big ask, especially if we're best friends, like you claim. I just don't want you to lie to me. Is it that complicated?"

In that moment Nicky wanted to tell Josie everything, to share it all, whatever she could do to bring back that softness. To tell her not only that she missed her, missed hugging her, and hearing about what was going through her head, but also about the trees. That she could hear them, and that they had a message for her. They *needed* her, and this meant—she understood it now—that she needed them, and her sister as well.

She still didn't know what she, a new person to Alaska,

could do to stop a town from voting to cut the trees, or halt an army of chainsaws led by Uncle Cliff and Sven's brother. But she knew that together, she and Josie could be powerful. They could solve this problem.

Before Nicky could say any of this, Josie disappeared into the television room.

Nicky turned to readjust the photo of the three-masted ship behind her. Then she went into the attic to change out of her wet clothes, making sure to select a long-sleeve shirt to cover her wrists so her father wouldn't see the scratches left from the thorns on the devil's club. When she came back down, Josie was drinking a glass of water at the table, watching her warily as she crossed the room to pour one of her own.

"How's Clete?" her father asked. "Is he as good as Uncle Cliff at driving that skiff?"

She inhaled, glancing at Josie, who watched her. If she was going to tell a lie, she knew she'd need to commit to it.

"He's better than his dad. He knows all sorts of places for otter, and sea lions. We saw anemones and starfish. He told me the names of different seaweeds, and which were good to eat."

"Oh yeah? I was thinking maybe we should buy a little skiff for ourselves. You guys could learn to drive like proper Alaska girls. Or we could get kayaks, and paddle to some of the nearby islands." Nicky took a seat at the table and stared out the window, watching the light dim over Sven's rusted metal roof, ignoring the burn of Josie's eyes.

"Nicky, I'm so proud of you," her father continued.

"Having the courage to go out on the water like that and explore. I don't think any of us are going to be happy here without getting out of our comfort zones. I know it's difficult not to be able to walk around in the forest. After this big vote on Friday Cliff said he'd be happy to go out with us, and he'll bring a firearm for bears. Which reminds me: Uncle Cliff gave us some freshly harvested toppings. Let's get this pizza in the oven."

Nicky snuck a glance at her sister, who clacked down her empty water glass and stared at her with unblinking eyes. *Go away,* Nicky thought.

To her surprise, Josie stood.

"I need to work on my speech for Wednesday. Let me know when dinner's ready."

"It's ready," their father said, holding three balls of dough wrapped in plastic. He tossed one to Josie, who caught it. His movements were lighthearted. He seemed happy, like a great weight had been removed. She knew how angry he would be if he ever discovered that his daughter was lying to him.

"My speech is in three days, and I feel like no one in this house is taking it seriously," Josie said as she sifted flour over the table for her dough, just like their mother had taught them.

"J, we just spent a good part of today going over it."

"Until you got all dressed up to go to the tree slaughter-house."

"It's called a lumber mill," he said, settling at the table and rolling dough beneath his palms.

"What are the toppings?" Nicky asked. Suddenly she was starving.

"Venison, and some of the season's first winter chanterelles, which your uncle picked while cruising the timber up in Sky River Valley. This is pickled bull kelp Aunt Mall made. How's that for some pioneer pizza?"

"Blech," Josie said, refilling her glass at the sink. "Why can't we just do cheese and sauce like the rest of the world?"

"The rest of the world eats pepperoni, unlike you," their father said. "Wash your hands."

Josie turned off the water and returned to the table. "That's not true. People are starting to realize we can't keep taking from the earth. That includes deer, and mushrooms."

Nicky's father dropped her dough in front of her. "Your uncle spent a lot of time in the woods gathering these mushrooms and processing this animal. I know you don't eat meat, but you should at least try the chanterelles."

"Sorry. No earth resources for me."

Their father threw his hands up. "I don't know where to start. Where do you think cheese, and tomatoes, and wheat come from?" he said, his voice rising. Then he turned to Nicky, reaching for her wrist. "And what about these scratches? Where'd *they* come from?" he asked.

"Oh," she said, snatching her arm back and pulling down the cuff of her sweatshirt. "Clete and I found some anemones down in the tide pools. They're all spiky."

"Did Clete say you could eat those too?" Josie asked, her voice heavy with sarcasm. "I mean, that's amazing. He knows so much. What about some of this bull kelp?" Josie said, using her fingers to pick a shred of green from the bowl. "Did you guys come across this today? Why doesn't Clete start a wild foods delivery? That way, his dad wouldn't have to cut down all the trees."

Nicky rested her eyes on her sister. "Why are you so annoying?"

Josie went red. "Me? You're the one who's annoying. You're like a lost chameleon, trying to blend into a place where you don't belong—and you know you never will."

"Girls." Their father exhaled. "Please. I just want to have a nice Sunday evening."

Nicky gnawed at the insides of her cheeks as she glared back at her sister. Her bangs had brightened, and she realized that Josie had dyed her hair again—this time even greener, like the spruce needles around town. Probably in response to Aunt Mall's promise to fix the color.

She didn't want to fight with Josie. She also hated the feeling of giving any ground to her sour mood, letting it infect everything and everyone around her. Even if all she really wanted to do was eat cheesy pizza, climb the stairs to the attic, and flop down on her bed and cuddle up with Josie and tell her everything. To allow her sister's straightforward, methodical mind to sort through the evidence and show her the way out of the maze she felt caught inside.

"Your sister's speech is a good one," their father said as he used a palm to flatten out the dough. "She doesn't miss a beat. She almost had me convinced that those trees shouldn't be cut."

Nicky turned to her father. "Almost?"

He spooned on red sauce, and shook his head. "Those guys out at the mill, not to mention Uncle Cliff—they depend on lumber for their jobs. This pandemic has left folks here shaken. It's hard for people to put food on the table."

"Why don't they just go out and get mushrooms and shoot deer, like Uncle Cliff?" Josie suggested.

"Some of them probably are doing just that," their father said, not registering—or ignoring—Josie's sarcasm.

"Wait. So you agree with Uncle Cliff?" Nicky said incredulously. "You're going to vote to clear-cut the valley?"

Their father put his hands up, laughing in a lighthearted way that made Nicky want to fling her dough in his face. "Easy, Nick. I'm not sure if I can take both of you angry at me at the same time. First of all, I don't have a vote, because we're not residents. But yes, if I could vote, I would probably vote to cut the valley. There are millions of acres of trees left in the forest. This is only a few hundred. I don't see a reason why those trees should survive, while people like your uncle should be forced off the island, searching for work."

Anger spread like a fire through Nicky. She didn't know what to say, or where to start. It felt like a betrayal, like ground she had been sure of, and depended on, was suddenly falling away from beneath her.

"You're just like the rest of them, aren't you?" Josie said. "Putting yourself in front of the earth, not even considering that *we're* the ones who are going to be picking up your path of destruction. Nicky and me and the rest of our generation."

He took off his glasses, letting them hang around his

neck. He inhaled until his shirt strained at the buttons. "I understand the two of you are passionate. But these things are complicated. It's not simple, needing to support a family."

"Mom was the doctor, not you," Josie snapped. "She was the one who supported our family."

"Enough!" Their father stood, his face as red as his hair, knocking back the table, toppling the bowls. He slammed his fist down on the wood. Josie's dough rose into the air, hovering for a moment, before slapping the floor. Both girls stared up at him. Nicky had never seen his face so pinched, his eyes so small. He looked like a monster. "You two have no idea how much your mother and I struggled before either of you were around. No idea! *I* supported her through the toughest of times. *I* was the one working with no rest."

After a moment he calmed. "I'm—I'm sorry," he stammered. "I'm sorry."

He left them in the kitchen. Josie slowly picked up her dough, dropped it in the trash can, and went upstairs. Nicky observed the scattered toppings, then reached for a mushroom, expecting the smallest of currents. Nothing.

After a moment, she spread sauce on her dough, picked cheese and mushrooms, venison, and even a few shreds of kelp from the mess on the table, and slipped her pizza into the oven. She was starving. So she would eat alone.

CHAPTER EIGHTEEN

Three days later, Nicky woke to find her sister's bed already made. Sun streamed in, even though the boardwalk below was dark with rain. The trees in Sky River Valley seemed to float on their trunks. A few eagles flapped lazily against the blue sky. She rose from her bed, already eager to get outside and soak up the sunshine, as far as she could get from the awkward silence in their house. She made a note to remind Clete about the bike he said he'd bring her.

When Nicky came downstairs, she glimpsed Josie on the computer in the front room. Veronica waved at her on the screen, and Nicky waved back. "Hi!" she said. She heard Veronica say, "See you at the town hall tonight!" before Josie rose and shut the door, making a face at her.

In the kitchen, her father wore his red glasses on the tip of his nose as he flipped through *The Jackson Cove Caller* while sipping his coffee.

"Morning, kiddo," he said, putting down the paper. She opened the fridge for milk and didn't answer. Just a plastic bottle of orange juice, a can of ready-to-bake biscuits, a jar of jelly and peanut butter, and her dad's crusty ball of dough left over from Sunday's pizza night.

"Sorry for the empty fridge," her dad said. "I'm a bad hunter. Aunt Mall should be by any minute to drop off groceries."

"It's okay. I'm not that hungry."

He tapped the newspaper. "It says in here that there's going to be social distancing when the middle school opens in a couple weeks. Hygiene stations, testing twice a month. That means you kids will be wearing masks in the classroom."

Josie stepped into the kitchen. "I'm not going to school in a mask," she announced, pulling out her earbuds. "In fact, I might not go to school at all. Veronica and I were just talking about building our own learning pod. Her parents think it's a good idea. Her dad, Nathan, says schools are an invention of the Industrial Revolution, to occupy children while their parents work in the factories. He doesn't believe in them. Veronica says we're probably the smartest in middle school—no offense, Nicky. Her mother might reach out to you, Dad. They're thinking of flying a Native teacher up from Metlakatla, where Veronica's mother grew up, so we can learn the Tsimshian language."

"I can't even keep track of half of what you're saying, but as far as I know, you still owe your sister an apology for Sunday night."

"Don't get me started on who owes who an apology,"

Josie said. "Are you coming to my speech tonight?" she asked, eyeing Nicky.

"Maybe."

"You have to come," Josie said matter-of-factly. "It would look pathetic if my own sister wasn't there."

Her father folded the newspaper. "I'm going to listen on the radio. People will be more comfortable that way, considering that we haven't been here fourteen days. And I think I should give you some space."

Josie watched him warily. "Space? Why would I need space? Now you're distancing from *us*?"

"Nooo . . . ," he said, smiling. "You'll knock it out of the park tonight. I'll be just up the street."

Josie held his stare, then let it go. She poured herself a glass of orange juice. "All I know is that I'm going to speak my mind, and take action, just like Mom would have. She never sat around doing nothing. She did what was right."

"Josie," her father said, sounding tired. "Please don't get started again. We're all doing what we think is right."

"This isn't a time for being comfortable," she persisted. "Or for being scared. When you see something that's wrong, you speak up." She gulped down her orange juice and set her dirty glass in the sink with a clack. "You use reason, and logic, and tell others how to get better. That's what Mom would have done. So that's what I'm doing."

Their father picked up his guitar and slide. "As I said before, I'm proud of you. Your speech will be great."

"Please don't play too loud," Josie said. "Veronica and I

are about to do online yoga. We both have to clear our heads for the town hall." And she left.

Nicky sat alone. She needed to tell her sister about the trees. Even if Josie made fun of it, she needed to tell her that she had felt something. Sky River Valley could speak. This was about more than saving a forest. It was about saving lives.

Resolving not to give up until she broke through Josie's icy exterior, Nicky went down the wood-clad hall and opened the door to the front room. Josie sat cross-legged on her purple mat, staring forward at the wall. Her computer was closed behind her.

"Hey," Nicky said. Josie didn't budge. "Did you already feed Watermelon?"

"Yes. Now please go." She continued to stare at the wall.

"Are you—meditating?" Nicky asked, taking a step forward. When Josie didn't respond, Nicky said, "I'll come tonight."

"Good. Please shut the door."

"Can I stay in here and talk to you?"

"No," her sister said flatly. "I already told you. I have a class scheduled, and I need to think through my speech."

"But you're just —"

Josie broke her stare-off with the wall, set her hands on her knees, and turned to face her sister. "Please get out of the room and leave me alone. Now."

Nicky shut the door quietly. She moved past the kitchen, where mournful notes rose from her father's guitar. She went downstairs, guiding the door shut behind her. Standing on the damp boardwalk, she breathed in the moist air, closing her eyes as her lungs filled and fighting back tears.

Meooowwww.

Rooster stood in Sven's doorway, arching her back and rubbing it against a peeling wooden post holding up the portico. The cat inspected Nicky with her large, golden eyes.

"Oh, Rooster," Nicky said, wiping her tears with her coat sleeve. "I wish you could tell me what I'm supposed to do."

From an open window Nicky heard the pluck of Sven playing his mandolin. He sang softly about a salesman who lost his way while traveling between towns.

Rooster continued to watch her.

"What?"

The cat dashed off, her tail high as she slipped behind the toolshed.

Nicky started down the gravel road. At the end of it she breathed in the sea air, trying to quiet her mind. Telling herself, over and over, again and again, that no matter what happened to those trees, everything would be okay. And not believing it for one second.

That evening, she left her father at the kitchen table with the radio beside him, its metal antenna stretched into the air. He looked like someone in the movies, with one ear glued to the shiny box. Nicky thought of these waves connecting each of the houses on the island, just like the fungal networks joining the tree roots in Sky River Valley. Creating a community that prospered, or went down, together. When the signal got scratchy, he touched the antenna, though the radio station was just across Main Street, down the road from the town hall.

"Tell your sister good luck for me," he said as Nicky went down the stairs. "I'm here listening."

"I'll tell her."

The buildings cast long shadows in the setting sun across Main Street. The windows of the Ben Franklin Store advertised HOME SCHOOL KITS with math books and do-it-yourself science labs, with pictures on the posters of children smiling over microscopes. Nicky wondered how many kids would actually show up this year for school. Like Josie, she didn't want to wear a mask in class, or be confined to her own particular quadrant, protected by a plastic barrier. She also didn't want to deal with the other kids thinking she was infected because she came from the Lower 48, or because her mother had died from the virus.

The town hall was a low-slung building situated along the water. As Nicky crossed the street toward it, she saw Clete and Uncle Cliff coming up from the harbor, looking like twins in their flannels and jeans and brown XtraTufs. Clete wheeled a bike beside him. Aunt Mall wasn't with them. Nicky wore her boots too, the rubber molded to her feet. Even if it wasn't raining, or if she wasn't going to the woods, she loved how the boots felt. The Jackson Cove Slippers made her feel protected from the rain and mud, and also like she belonged on this island.

From across the parking lot she waved. Clete waved

back. They met in front of a bronze statue of a small, bald man with a hand on his knee, gazing west over the ocean.

"Hey, Nicky. Is your sister speaking tonight?" Clete asked.

"Yes," Nicky responded, watching as Uncle Cliff lifted his mesh hat and patted down his dark black hair.

Uncle Cliff sighed. "I'm afraid your sister and I, we're going to be speaking on different sides of the aisle," he said as he examined the brown-shingled building by the water. "I don't like to speak against family. I hope she doesn't hold it against me."

"She will," Nicky assured him, barely containing her own anger at the thought of Uncle Cliff leading a crew of loggers into Sky River Valley, where he had just shot a deer and gathered mushrooms.

"I understand her worry for the future of the planet. And yours. But I'm afraid she can't just step onto this island and tell people how to act. It doesn't work like that. People are desperate for jobs. C'mon. Let's go in."

"Nicky, I'll leave the bike here for you," Clete said, leaning it against the building. "So you can get around town if you need to."

"Thanks."

Uncle Cliff held the door for them. As they walked in, Clete whispered, "That's so you can get into the valley." This confused her. He had said when they went into the woods that she could use it to explore town. She couldn't imagine going into Sky River Valley without him, especially considering the bears. She didn't even have pepper spray.

Display cases in the lobby showed dusty sea otters and land otters, robes made of ground squirrel and marten skins, and coats stitched from seal and sea lion fur. High above, a halibut with its mouth open to a wooden hook was carved into a slab of yellow cedar. Next to it was an oil painting of the same cranky-looking bald man whose statue was outside, the Russian who had led the battle against the Tlingits in 1804.

A tall older man with sun-bleached, sandy blond-and-pewter hair approached Cliff. "Hey, guy," he said. His low voice echoed in the lobby. He had tortoiseshell glasses and wore loafers with tassels and no socks. "You have your speech prepared?"

"Evening, Lars," Uncle Cliff said. "I'm not much for preparing speeches, but I've got a few words I'll share."

"Good, Cliff. I'm sure that'll be fine. What do you think our Russian friend would think of all this?" Lars said, tipping his head at the painting.

"I think he'd be kicking himself for not getting the rest of those trees out of the valley," Cliff said, observing instead the yellow cedar carving of the halibut.

This made Lars laugh. "You're right, aren't you? He wanted what you and I do, to help develop this island. Make it a place suitable for people to live."

"Lars, this here's my niece Nicky Hall," Uncle Cliff said. "And look who's coming over. This is my other niece, Josephine."

Josie met eyes with Nicky as she crossed the lobby. She had tied her curls back in two tight buns that resembled small unripe pumpkins. Tendrils of green hair fell like vines to either side of her eyes. She wore a hooded rose-colored dress that their mother had bought for her two years ago, for a father-daughter dance at Danville Elementary School. The dress fit too tightly now, and seemed wildly out of place among the worn jeans and XtraTufs and oiled baseball caps in the crowd.

Josie clearly didn't care. Nicky felt the familiar pang of envy, wishing she had her sister's confidence, as Josie glared up at the tall owlish man, who blinked back at her from behind his round glasses.

"Hi, little miss. I hear you'll be speaking against cutting the valley tonight, along with my brother, I suspect. I admire your pluck."

"I don't admire *you*," Josie retorted. "After tonight, I hope your mill gets shut down."

Lars's bushy eyebrows shot up, and his thin lips shrank into his mouth. "I hope, for the sake of this island, and your uncle and your father, that it doesn't."

Josie watched him. "Our father will be fine without your mill. So will Cliff. His family has been living here for thousands of years without clearcutting. Right, Uncle Cliff?"

They all turned to him. Nicky had never seen her uncle at a loss for words. "My family has been finding their own way on Shee for some time," he finally said.

"Unlike your family, who arrived less than a week ago, right?" Lars said. "And already your father has a job at the mill. That is, so long as we get that valley."

Uncle Cliff sighed. He shot a look at Lars, then hooked

his thumbs into the pockets of his jeans, squared his shoulders to the group, and examined the carpet beneath him.

"Well, pleasure to meet you girls," Lars said, stepping away. "I guess I better go see if I can't find a place to stand."

"Uncle Cliff, what was he talking about?" Josie said when the tall man left.

"Josie, I'm sorry he didn't tell you two, but your dad's been interviewing with us. He'll be helping to find buyers for the old growth we'll be logging—the higher-end wood. He's got great people skills. Your dad's an impressive guy." Uncle Cliff gestured with his chin at the room. "Should we make a move?"

Nicky started inside, but Josie grabbed her wrist.

"Did you know any of this?"

Nicky shook her head. She watched as her sister's face began to fall. Then Josie collected herself and knit her brow, as if to freeze any tears that might start. Her face clouded over, and her lips tightened. "I wish the virus had gotten him instead of Mom," she said.

Before Nicky could respond, Josie marched toward the main hall, the cowl hood on her red dress flowing like a cape behind her.

PART FOUR

The Fight for the Trees

CHAPTER NINETEEN

"Citizens of Jackson Cove, please find a place. As you can see, we're using the main hall to give everyone space. We have seats up front for the newspaper and radio reporters, as well as for the disabled and our elders. The rest of you are welcome to stand, so long as you keep six feet distance. No one will be admitted without a mask. We have a lot to get through tonight, and Jackson KOVE is standing by, so please let's not waste our time."

It was Alice, Nicky saw, the same woman who had yelled at them at the harbor a couple nights earlier, speaking from behind the lectern at the front of the room. She wore her salmon mask over her mouth, and her gray curls piled on her head.

Nicky saw Josie in a corner speaking with Veronica, the two of them wearing masks but still keeping distance. Veronica looked even more beautiful in person than she had in the video. She had creamy, windswept cheeks above her

167

Alaskan flag mask. She wore her hair in a ponytail, and dark blue jeans with the cuffs folded. The couple close to her must have been her parents, well-dressed and speaking with their foreheads almost touching. Her mother had her black hair pulled back and wore a poncho-like cape with a crest embroidered onto it.

Nicky considered going over and introducing herself, especially after Veronica had mentioned meeting at the town hall over the computer. Then she saw Uncle Cliff wave to her from the side of the room. She made her way forward, thinking that now wasn't the best time to meet her sister's new best friend.

She passed a woman sitting at a table of equipment, wearing headphones, then felt a tug on her windbreaker. "Hey, love!" It was Aunt Mall stretching out a long arm to bridge the distance between them.

"Hi, Aunt Mall."

"You ready for your sister's big moment?"

Nicky nodded. Clete waved, and she joined her cousin and uncle against the wall. In front of her, Nicky saw Sven, in oil-splattered blue jeans, his yellow hat hanging from a string around his neck. Rooster purred away in his lap. The cat looked over and blinked lazily at her, not even flinching as Alice's gavel came down with a *thwack!*

"Everyone, thank you for taking time out of your busy schedules to come to this evening's town hall and thank you to those listeners with us on Jackson KOVE, and watching over Zoom. Especially with so much worry over the virus, when so many of us would prefer to be out on our boats fishing, picking chanterelles, walking the dog, or enjoying the last of the warm weather before the fall storms hit. We appreciate your presence here tonight, virtual or otherwise. I see everyone in here is wearing masks, and I thank you."

Nicky wondered where this calm, collected woman had been the night she yelled at them by the harbor.

"I know tempers have been flaring," Alice continued, as if answering Nicky's thoughts. "In the grocery store aisles, on the docks, even down at the bars. I also know that everyone in this room loves the island where we live, and we all think we know what's best for it. Our job tonight will be to set those thoughts aside, and to listen. Rage has no place here. In order to survive, we need to trust one another. We don't live like the Lower 48. We can't just drive off and get away. There are ten miles of road—the rest is rock, ice, and trees. This vote coming up on Friday is about the trees. It's also about hearing one another, and putting others in front of ourselves. Along with us adults speaking, we're going to have Veronica Deschumel and her friend, a newcomer to Shee Island, give a speech."

"Everyone knows whose side they're on," someone grumbled. "Don't see why we have to sit through it."

"Because these two girls have the guts to stand up here and talk about it," a voice Nicky recognized growled back. It was Sven's.

"Up to the microphone with you if you'd like to share," Alice snapped. "Three minutes. State your name."

Uncle Cliff stepped forward, his hands shoved in his

pockets as he made his way carefully around the chairs to the front of the room.

"Good evening," he said. The microphone whined, sending feedback into the speakers. Alice leaned over to adjust it to account for their height difference. "Kéet yóo xat duwasáakw ku.aa Dleit Káa X'éináx Cliff McCleod. My Tlingit name is Kéet, and my English name is Cliff McCleod. Gooch naax xat sitee. I belong to the Wolf clan. Yéil naax siteeyín ax éesh. I'm a child of the Raven moiety. Yáax' yéi xat yatee. Jackson Cove-x'. I live here, in Jackson Cove."

He took a deep breath and swallowed. The crowd was silent. Nicky turned to Clete, and whispered, "Do you also speak Tlingit?"

He smiled back at her and leaned close. "S'áaxwshaan and my grandmother tried to teach me. It's hard."

"Ladies and gentlemen, I'll be brief," Uncle Cliff said. "This is not a difficult equation we have in front of us. If the mill where I work as crew foreman isn't given access to the big timber in Sky River Valley, then this town is done for. It's as simple as that. At least, the town for working people and families. It will become a place for rich people from Seattle and Juneau and Anchorage to build second homes, especially those wishing to escape the city as a result of this pandemic. The people who live and work here, the majority of people in this room, will be priced out. I will need to move my family down south. Jackson Cove will be transformed, and not in a way that I believe my parents, and their parents before them, and their parents before them, would appreciate."

He stared over the crowd, nodding slightly.

"This island where I grew up, where I married, where I had my boy—this place is special. Spiritual. My ancestors knew it, just as the Russians knew it when they first crashed on our shores. They wanted to enslave us, to force us to hunt otter for them, as they had with the Aleut and Aleutiq tribes up north. History has noted how the Tlingits stood up for themselves and for their way of life on this island. Katlian, a Tlingit war chief, fought the man cast in bronze outside this town hall. After the Russians left, the anthropologists from universities arrived, wanting to study this island, to make a record of our language and our ways of subsistence. In more recent years, people have been coming by boat or plane to shoot our brown bear and catch our salmon. In short, to take. Now, with this pandemic ravaging the world, we find ourselves at a turning point. Cities in the Lower 48, and across the world, empty out as people search for community, for a more pure, and simple way of life. People realize that we have food up here, from the forest and the sea. We also have peace, because we are self-sufficient. We don't need others, because we have the resources to sustain ourselves and our families."

Uncle Cliff gripped the sides of the lectern and dropped his head. He breathed in, then looked up again.

"People on this island know me. They know my uncle S'áaxwshaan, and the stories he told of the Lady and the Volcano. They know my parents, and my grandparents. We have always been in favor of subsisting on what we have, rather than inviting others to ruin it. This approach to life only becomes more necessary at times like these. We cannot continue to encourage people to come to our island, even if it means jobs. Because it's putting ourselves, and our children, at risk. We need to keep ourselves safe, and our children safe. I do not want people arriving by plane from Seattle and even Japan or wherever else. We have had not one case of Covid-19 on this island. I want to keep it that way. We know that the flu in 1918 all but destroyed many of the Native villages in this state. Let's band together in this tough moment, hunker down, and protect. If we are allowed to cut Sky River Valley, this will give us another five years at least of running the mill, to sustain us while this virus passes. We will be able send wood out rather than bring tourists in, who might be sick. I don't want to be the one who, after ten thousand years of my family on Shee, has to look my boy in the eye and tell him that we put his island in danger. Or—worse—that we have to leave the island home that we built with our own two hands. Don't make me be this person. Please vote in favor of cutting Sky River Valley, to allow us, as community members of Jackson Cove, to continue our way of life by working with the land, in the mill, without putting ourselves and our children in danger. Gunalchéesh, yéi áwé. Thank you. That is all."

Uncle Cliff threaded through the room as it erupted in applause. From the back of the room, Lars yelled, "Here, here!"

Across from her, Sven rose, walked to the lectern, and turned to face the audience. Rooster crouched on his shoulder, surveying the crowd with his golden eyes.

"Most of you know me as that crabby old fisherman with

the black cat who doesn't talk to no one, but my name is Sven Ruger," he said. "I have no silver tongue, at least not like my friend who spoke before me, or my brother, Lars, in the back there." He lifted his chin in a sarcastic gesture of greeting.

"Great-grandfather Ruger arrived here more recently than Cliff's kin, back in the 1850s, chased out of Norway for religion. And I'll tell you one thing: he didn't come searching for a land where people told him what to do. No siree. Anyone who's ever gone up against my brother knows as much. But I been back to Norway. You go into the hills, the first thing you notice—there's hardly a tree left. They don't have no more wild salmon because all they do is farm fish. They messed it up—all of it. Their mountains as well as their streams and oceans. Let me tell you, folks. I stare out at them trees every night before sleep, thanking them for the work they do to give us the salmon that keep me and Rooster busy. Thanking them for the work they do breathing for us, sending us oxygen. That old yellow cedar out there, it's been making a nursery for the salmon for well over a thousand years. In fact, those trees do just what Mr. McCleod was discussing—allow us to subsist without the help of others. I'm sure your ancestors weren't in favor of mowing down a bunch of forest that made sure you had fish to put up in the fall," Sven said, looking at Cliff. Rooster arched his back as Sven reached up to pet the cat.

"Now, my ancestors from Norway came here to find a place in the gloom where they didn't have to answer to no kings knocking on their door telling them how to pray.

Where people could do as they wanted. But I'll tell you, what we've come up against here is something larger than we can control. Like it or not, we're experiencing climate change. I see it every day out on the water, catching tuna alongside salmon as the oceans warm. We're in some sort of hurry to chop down the trees that breathe for us? It makes about as much sense as reaching in with a knife and slicing out our own lungs.. The forest and the fish depend on each other. My brother knows it, but he's just too darned stubborn and scared, and greedy, to make a change. One look at his house up there on that rock tells you as much. Don't do it. Save these trees. That's all I have to say about that."

As Sven limped away from the lectern, a few people clapped, including Nicky. Though she had to admit, he didn't speak as powerfully as Uncle Cliff did.

"Okay. Thank you, Mr. Ruger. I'd like to invite Veronica and her guest, Josephine Hall, up to the podium."

Veronica's parents clapped as she and Josie made their way forward. Veronica moved with the same self-assurance she had shown in that video they saw on the ferry. Her father, who had chestnut skin and close-cropped silvery hair, squeezed Veronica's wrist as she passed. Her mother took down the hood of her poncho and said something to Veronica, who nodded and smiled.

As the two girls approached the front of the room, the woman from the radio fooled with a few knobs, then nodded at Alice. Her father's decision to stay back at the house made no sense to Nicky. She shut her eyes and wished, with all of

174

her heart, for her mother to appear somewhere in the room, cheering on Josie just as she cheered the Ironmen baseball team, loud and obnoxious.

At the podium, Josie and Veronica squared their shoulders to the silent room. Alice brought a step stool over so that Josie could match Veronica's height.

"Good evening, Jackson Cove," Veronica said in a rich, smooth voice. The rolled cuffs of her jeans just touched the tops of the swirl of the pastel octopus legs on her turned-down XtraTufs. "I'd like to offer a warm welcome to all present. As many of you know, I am a seventh-grader at Shee Middle School, and I run the Drama, Debate, & Forensics Club. My father helps with Jackson Cove Convos, and my mother makes traditional Tsimshian clothing. I'm proud to live here in Jackson Cove. I've spoken on behalf of the youth for so many of these events. Tonight, I'd like to make an exception and introduce my new friend Josephine Hall, who arrived here last week. She is from Pennsylvania, and has come here with her father and her twin sister, Nicky." Veronica gave a friendly wave to Nicky, accompanied by a smile. "Josie and Nicky are nieces of Mallory and Cliff McCleod, as I think many of you know."

People around the room clapped as Veronica stepped aside. Josie leaned forward and angled the microphone toward her.

"Thank you, Jackson Cove, and Veronica." Josie's voice was soft. Nicky's heart revved, and her palms began to sweat. She watched as Josie's fingers fumbled with her phone. Josie prided herself on memorizing her speeches, and never, ever, read them. Something was wrong. Josie lifted her head to face the crowd again.

"Thank you to my friend Veronica for letting me speak to you about this important issue facing Shee Island today. I'd like to speak on the subject of deforestation, which is when we log our natural forests. We cut down trees to make land for housing, and to get wood. This creates jobs, just like my uncle said before."

Nicky stole a glance at her uncle. He stood with his back straight, wearing a serious expression as he watched Josie.

"The mill at the end of the road needs wood to continue to work. We understand that. The problem is that the earth is running out of forests to log. Especially the older trees, like the ones in Sky River Valley that Mr. Ruger spoke of. These trees take the carbon dioxide we breathe and give us back oxygen. The forests also create an important habitat for whitetail deer, bear, mountain goats, and salmon, like Mr. Ruger said."

"Mountain goats don't need trees," someone scoffed.

"No whitetail deer here either."

Alice hissed at the crowd. "Quiet!"

Josie looked down at her phone again. "As many of you know, trees cover almost one-third of the globe. By cutting the trees in Sky River Valley down, we disrupt critical water cycles, accelerating soil erosion and climate change." She picked her head up from the phone. "Plus, even if the mill where my uncle works closes, there are other things people can do. Seattle isn't far. Tech jobs don't require anyone to cut trees. That's an obvious one. Humans are built to improvise and dream up different ways of doing things. For example, you can make things on Etsy out of shells you find on the beach, and pine cones."

Josie's voice sounded squeaky. Her eyes scanned the crowd and met Nicky's. Never had Josie looked so scared and unsure. Nicky regretted not standing beside her in the back of the room, even with Veronica there.

"When there's overpopulation, then houses require heating, and people cut the forest. Land is also cleared for livestock as people demand milk and meat products."

A deep voice chimed in from the back of the room. "Only two thousand people, and no cows or pigs on the island." It was Lars.

Uncle Cliff swiveled around. "Hey. She's a kid. Lighten up."

People shifted. Alice took a step closer to the podium. Nicky could see from Josie's expression that she knew the speech wasn't going well. Lars had rattled her with his heckling, and his news of their father.

Josie straightened her back and lifted her chin. "In conclusion, forests like the one in Sky River Valley are the lungs of the earth. Just like the fishermen said, who slices out their lungs? No one. That's who. So neither should you. Thank you."

She stepped down, ducked her head, and walked toward the back of the room. Veronica trailed behind, her brightness gone. If her sister had never been embarrassed before in her life, then this was her first time. As Josie passed by her, Nicky reached out to squeeze her wrist, as Veronica's mother had done for her. Josie brushed by, knocking her hand out of the way.

"Thank you, Veronica and Josephine," Alice said. "Let's take a break before hearing from a couple more folks. Please remember that the vote is two days away, on Friday. Come here to cast your ballots. Let's meet back in fifteen minutes."

Uncle Cliff rose, and so did Clete and Nicky. At the back of the room Nicky saw Josie rip out her buns and head for the door. Veronica took off after her. In the lobby, Josie shoved open the glass doors and stepped into the night, with her new best friend close behind.

CHAPTER TWENTY

It was fully dark by the time Nicky left the town hall. She picked up the bike Clete had leaned against the wall and pedaled across the parking lot, past the bronze statue of the Russian man who killed otters and fought the Tlingit hero Katlian, and through town's single stoplight, which blinked yellow this late at night. Past the harbor, then up the gravel road.

Nicky slipped the bike into a shed behind the house, peering up at their kitchen window. A shadow moved across the wall. A moment later she heard her father's guitar.

She went around front and opened the door. Josie's shoes were nowhere to be seen. She climbed the stairs, then stopped in the kitchen doorway to listen to her father sing.

Hard time is here, everywhere you go,
Times are harder than ever been before.

In the reflection of the glass Nicky watched her father's face contort as he ran his slide along the fret board, coaxing out the powerful sounds. He held the guitar close against his chest, as if to fend off sadness. Sitting in the dim light, playing guitar, letting his mind go where it needed to be—she knew he needed music to move through his sadness. But tonight, she needed him to talk to her.

"Hey, Dad," she started.

He startled, sitting up straight and swinging around in his chair. "Oh! Hey, it's you. God, you snuck up on me. What's happening, kiddo?"

"Not much," she said.

He strummed lightly on the strings, staring back out the window. "Where's Josie?"

"She left with Veronica," Nicky answered.

"Oh?" He stopped strumming.

"Dad," Nicky started. "Did you get a job at the mill?"

He set his guitar down on the couch. "Who told you that?"

"Lars Ruger. The owner."

"Oh," he repeated. "I was going to tell you girls this weekend. I just—your sister had been practicing so hard for her speech. I didn't want to ruin it. I knew she'd be angry."

"She thinks you lied to her," Nicky said.

He dropped his head and held the bridge of his nose between his fingers. "Of course she would think that. Why does she hate me so much?"

"The speech," Nicky started. "I stood with Uncle Cliff and Clete because they waved me over. Veronica's parents were there, but you weren't. I didn't stand with her. Then Uncle Cliff wanted people to vote to cut, and I would have felt weird just standing by myself—"

"I know."

"—then after Josie's speech she slapped my hand back when she passed. I just wanted, more than anything, Mom to be there. You know, yelling for Josie like she yelled at baseball games, all loud, calling the other team names."

Her father rose, crossed the room, and held her, stroking her head as she sobbed against his chest. Her vision blurred with her tears. She didn't know if she was crying because it felt like she was losing her sister, or her father, or the trees that kept trying to reach out to her. Then she felt his body heave, and she realized he was crying too. She had never seen her father cry.

"I'm sorry," he said. "I'm sorry. I should have come. I keep messing up. I just didn't want to embarrass your sister."

Nicky pulled away to watch him. She couldn't believe it, her father with tears coming down his ruddy cheeks. "I thought things were supposed to get easier in Alaska," she breathed.

"They *are* getting easier," he insisted. "We've just all had a tough run of it. I just keep doing the wrong thing. Sometimes, Nicky, I feel like I don't have the tools your mother did. It's like I'm searching as hard as I can, and I can't figure out the right move. And I'm realizing, it's because I never had to, because your mother always did it for me."

His hands shook as he stroked her hair. He gripped her and held her to him.

"You know, your mother went to work just two weeks after giving birth to you guys. Did I ever tell you that? I remember being in that big old house of ours, alone, with the two of you looking up at me from your blankets, just staring with your big eyes. I was so scared of hurting you— you know, feeding you the wrong thing, or holding you the wrong way. I remember so well hearing your mother come up the driveway in her truck. It was the sweetest sound I ever heard. Then we were a team again. After that we got someone to help. I learned, of course. But that day I remember feeling so out of my depth."

"What does that mean?" Nicky asked.

"It means lost. Just totally, completely lost," he said. "Exactly like I feel now. Like everything I do gets me even more lost. Speaking of which, Josie won't answer my texts. Should I call Veronica's father? I think I have his number."

"Sure. She should be there. I'm going for a walk," Nicky said, wiping her eyes with the cuffs of her sweatshirt.

"Good. Okay. I'll apologize to your sister. Don't go too far."

His words, coming through his tears, sounded funny to her. As she went down the steps, she steadied herself against the walls. The world felt off-balance. She let gravity push her down the gravel road and lead her across the street to the harbor. She followed the curve of the sidewalk until the cement switched to mossy rocks leading out to the breakwater. She picked her way among the boulders in the dark, her XtraTufs gripping the slick shale. The sound of waves lapping grew louder as she got farther out. Swirls of seaweed eddied into the spaces between the rocks. An occasional roller sprayed her boots, making them shine.

At the end, where the boulders sloped back into the water, Nicky settled beneath the blinking red light Clete had pointed out on that first trip, just four days ago, the evening after they arrived. It felt like a moment from another lifetime.

The steel pillar felt cold and hard against her back. Sunbursts of seagull guano spotted the gray and gave off a soft scent of ammonia. She could feel the light hum of the electric box through her spine. Still she sat, breathing in the air, letting her eyes rove the water as they searched for the tufted island where Clete lived, on the other side of Eastern Channel.

After a moment she found it, and followed the faint shadow line cast by the new moon where the small river cut through the island. Where she had stood with Clete on the bridge he had built with his father, watching fish, just before she set her palms against the spruce. Glimpsing, for the smallest of moments, life inside a tree.

How could she even consider helping the valley when her own family was falling apart? Nicky knew that Josie would be furious at their father for a long time, if not forever. She also understood that he was telling her, with his story of their birth, that he was scared. Though when she thought through his story in her head, it didn't quite make sense. After all, he was the one who would pick them up from school and help them with homework. He was the one who dropped them off at ballet lessons, or at the softball field. He figured things out. It just took him some time. And probably, her mother charted the course for their family.

As Nicky looked over the ocean, she decided that she'd gladly give up any ability to hear these trees if it meant that her family would be whole again. She'd give up the whole valley, the island, all the forests on earth to have her mother back. To wake up in their old house that smelled of furniture polish. To scamper down the oak at the sound of her mother pulling up the driveway.

"Mom!" she shouted over the water. "Mom?"

The light above her head continued to blink, washing her boots and the rock where she sat in red. She could shout all she wanted, there was nothing to be done—not about her mother, or her father, or her sister—or even the forest. Just as Watermelon swallowed lettuce in great gulps, so bulldozers and trucks would take the valley up, chunk by chunk. When they reached the Old Yellow Cedar, with its strips of feathery bark, its knobbed branches draped in moss, they'd gas up their chainsaws and dip the bars into the lemony flesh. After a thousand years, it would fall like the rest of them. That was just what happened on earth. Trees stood tall, until they didn't.

Nicky slumped against the pillar. She slapped her palm down on the flat gray rock, just to feel the sting up her wrist, the vibrations moving into her shoulder. As she sat there, the hurt shifted into something else—the realization that you could depend on nothing in this world. Not even yourself. Not your sister, or father, or mother, or that the trees outside your window would be there when you woke. In less than a week, Alaska had taught her as much.

She had also learned that Aunt Mall was wrong. Nicky wasn't an Alaska girl. She wasn't strong enough to live in a place where things were in perpetual danger of falling apart, or—worse—disappearing altogether. At Uncle Max's you could always see the light of an open field between the trees. There was always a way out. She needed that. A forest with no end—she couldn't grasp it.

She clenched and unclenched her toes, watching as her jeans went red, then dark again. The ocean continued to push up against the rocks, rising and falling. And the light continued to blink, showing boats at sea the way home.

"I'm so happy to be here with my girls." That's what her mother would say as she stepped down from the running boards of her black pickup in the evening after work.

Nicky knew that her home was here, with her sister, and her father, and Aunt Mall, Uncle Cliff, and Clete. Still, she felt out of place, alone, and weak. Unable to meet anyone's demands or expectations, including the frightened trees of Sky River Valley.

Slowly, she rose. It was pitch dark now, and she took her time picking her way among the rocks and trudged up the hill toward the house, a step at a time. Pausing at the front door, before turning the scratched brass handle, and starting up the stairs.

CHAPTER TWENTY-ONE

O n Friday morning Nicky woke to the radio playing downstairs, and Josie pulling on her jeans and searching her bags.

"I can't find my fleece vest," she said. "Did you borrow it?"

"No," Nicky said. She strained to hear the words drifting up to her. It was a deep voice, one she recognized, discussing the vote on Sky River Valley.

Sun streamed through the open window. Today would mark their first week in Alaska. Brisk sea air blew in, ruffling the sheets.

"Where are you going?" Nicky asked as she got up to help her sister look for her vest. Neither of them had unpacked, and clothes were strewn all over the floor.

"To town hall, where people are voting. Veronica and two of her friends from DDF made 'Save Sky River Valley' signs. What do you think of mine?"

Josie pulled a two-by-four from alongside her bed and

held it up; attached to it was a piece of cardboard that said TAKE CARE OF YOUR CHILDREN: NO ON SKY RIVER.

Nicky squirreled through her bag for a fresh pair of jeans. "Can I come?" she asked, excited at the prospect of landing on a way to help the trees. "I can do a sign quickly. Maybe just 'Save the Valley' or 'Don't Cut Down Our Future.'"

Josie set her hands on her hips. "Whose side are you on? At the town hall you stood with Uncle Cliff. Now you're talking to Dad after he lied to us. And you want to make signs?"

"I already told you, J. I hadn't ever met Veronica, and I thought you guys were preparing for your speech. You made it clear she was your friend when you took that walk alone with her through Totem Park. I didn't want to interrupt. I had met Clete and Uncle Cliff outside, and they waved me over."

"Do you know what it's like to look out on the crowd and see your sister standing with the enemy?"

"He's our *uncle*. Not the enemy. Also, Dad didn't lie to us. He just didn't tell us."

"See? You're defending him. Nicky, you need to wake up. These adults, they've *screwed* us. Even Dad. Adults are self-ish enough to bring us into the world, then leave us gasping for life as they follow their own ambitions. They're *against* us. They *lie*, saying they want to keep us 'safe,' or that they're 'doing what's best for us.' They're so worried about money and the size of their house that they're willing to cut down trees that take hundreds of years to grow. What does that mean for you and me, and Veronica? For our children? We're left with nothing."

"I know, Josie. I know. Just please. Don't be so harsh with Dad."

"Dad . . . don't even get me started on him," Josie continued. "He didn't only lie to us. He betrayed mom too. She would have thrown up. She never lied. She also never ran away from a problem. The tragedy of it all is, whenever he makes another bad move, we're forced to go along with him just because we're not eighteen. That's so weird and arbitrary." Josie tore up lettuce, dropping leaves into Watermelon's tank. Then she grabbed her fleece from under her bed and zipped it to the neck. "Mom's not innocent either. She wanted to run that emergency room, so she kept going to work. What did that mean for us, her daughters? A life without a mother. Now we're just stuck following a man who really just wants to be left alone so he can build his stupid guitars."

"That's not kind."

"I DON'T CARE ABOUT BEING KIND!" her sister screamed from the top of the stairs. "Not one little bit."

They stared at one another. "I don't recognize you anymore," Nicky mumbled, turning to her bed and starting to make it.

"Your life is your life, Nicky," Josie said back. "At some point you're going to have to stop just standing around waiting to be struck by lightning. Waiting for someone to love you."

Before Nicky could respond, Josie charged down the

stairs, the wooden door rattling in its jamb as she slammed it behind her.

Nicky looked out her sister's window, watching Josie stride down the gravel road, hands shoved in her pockets. Another argument, another door slammed. When would it end? She climbed over to her bed, parting the curtains. The Old Yellow Cedar towered over the other trees, its fans of needles waving above the crowns of the hemlocks and spruce below. Her mind started to pick apart her sister's words, but then stalled out. She couldn't think. Nothing made sense anymore.

Nicky dressed and went downstairs. Her father sat exactly where she left him the night before, with his socked feet propped up on the windowsill. The only thing that had changed was that he was sipping coffee. He had turned the radio off. The newspaper lay spread on the table before him. JACKSON COVERS PREPARE TO VOTE ON FUTURE OF SKY RIVER VALLEY. Below it was a photo of the moss-covered forest, and a voting booth at town hall.

"Hey, honey," he said, turning around as she came in.

"Hey," Nicky said.

"Sounded like a blowout up there. You okay?"

"I don't know."

He stood and poured himself more coffee, shaking the old grounds into the trash.

"You want some of this?"

"I'm okay."

"Your sister's still not speaking to me."

"I figured."

"I heard Sven on the radio, asking people to vote no on cutting the valley. Seems like all siblings on the island are fighting." He nodded down at the paper. "I guess I better not start with Aunt Mall."

Nicky raised and dropped her shoulders.

"Are you mad at me too?" he asked.

She poured herself orange juice, then looked up at him, not knowing what to say. She *was* mad at him, but she also understood that things had not been easy. She understood he was doing his best. It just wasn't very good.

Her father pursed his lips and stared at her. "If people vote against the cut today, maybe that will solve the problem. We'll pile back up in the RV and head back to Danville. Would that make things better?"

Nicky shrugged, pouring granola. "Where would we live? You sold the house."

Her father pulled on his hat, adjusting the brim side-to-side as he looked out the window. "We could buy another one. I know people at the bank. It's just—hard," he continued. "Like you're trying to hear a tune, and you just can't quite make it out. I know there's a right way. It's just sticking around long enough to hear it."

Nicky wanted to tell him that he was their father. He should be able to not only hear that tune, but to follow it. Why was it so difficult for him?

"All of this feels like someone else's nightmare, doesn't it?" he asked her.

"Yes," she said softly, believing in her heart that the true nightmare was being a kid, like Josie said, and having a leader who had lost the way.

"I should have told you girls about the job," he said, looking back at her. "That much I know. Uncle Cliff made an unexpected offer the night we went out to the island. Then I met with him and Lars on Sunday, while you and Clete were out on the boat. Lars, he's actually a really nice guy. He wants what's best for the island, and also for our family."

Nicky didn't say anything.

"The mill—it's a way of life here. I want us to belong. I don't want to go back to Danville and be reminded of everything we lost. I want a new start. Lars Ruger has created a lot of opportunity on this island."

Nicky spooned yogurt into her granola, watching as the golden nuggets sunk into the soft white. "If you were a resident, would you really vote to cut down the trees?" she asked.

He settled back into his chair and recrossed his feet on the windowsill. When he didn't respond, she said, "I'm going for a bike ride."

She pulled on her windbreaker, then dragged the bike that Clete had brought her out from the back shed. She coasted down the gravel road, passing Sven's rusted pickup. At the harbor she turned left, letting the bike roll along the pavement. She climbed the hill past the boarding school where Clete's grandmother was punished for speaking Tlingit, then crossed the avenue, past the Alaska State Trooper Academy, where Clete might one day stand at attention beneath the American flag.

191

Her thighs burned as she pushed against the pedals. It felt good to move her legs and breathe in the ocean air. The world had stopped making sense, beginning with her sister, ending with her father, who didn't even seem able to answer a simple question. She still had this clean air, and her body, and her strong lungs. And for the moment, the trees in Sky River Valley were still breathing.

As she accelerated along the asphalt path built alongside of the road, the land opened up into an industrial area. Trailers, their metal sides coated in rust, with small gardens bordered by salt-splintered wooden fences, looked over the ocean. She pushed harder with her legs, squinting against the glare of the water.

The road curved into Henry's Bay. She passed the shipyard where they repaired the ferries that had brought her and her family to Alaska. A man welded outside, a shower of sparks rising from where he touched flame to metal. Another man shouted, then laughed, paying no attention as Nicky biked by. Now the road hugged the ocean, just a salt-rusted guardrail and a strip of fireweed separating asphalt from the glistening sea. She remembered the flowers Clete had given them a week ago. Just a few purple petals remained on the stalks, promising fall storms and a dark winter.

As she ran her eyes across the glassy surface of Eastern Channel, she saw a puff of air. The white cone went slack, and blurred as the breeze pulled the whale breath apart.

How thrilled she had been that first morning on the ferry when her father unzipped the tent and announced the humpback whale. This world was hers now. She could look onto the water and not be surprised to see a pod of whales feeding on herring just beyond the lighthouse. To see eagles floating on the currents above the treetops. Smell seaweed drying at low tide. She'd fight for this place, though she wasn't sure exactly what that meant.

She started up the hill toward Janie's Alley, where Veronica and her parents lived in a house over the water. Lars Ruger, Cliff's boss, soon to be her father's boss, had built his house on a cliff overlooking the ocean. As Nicky stood on the pedals of her bike, thrusting her legs, she could see the Ruger house, an octagon perched along the rocks. The windows blazed in the morning sun. It looked like a castle built over the ocean, ignoring the trees and forest at its back.

Lars had ambushed her sister's speech, she knew that now. Josie had been right when she said adults only care about money. Lars was the perfect example. Maybe he did care about the jobs, but he also didn't seem to care about the earth he'd leave behind when he died.

Flush with anger, Nicky considered turning off into his driveway to see if Lars was at home. She'd tell him all this to his face. She pedaled the rest of the way uphill, slowing when she reached the gravel road blasted through rock, leading to his house. Then she started peddling again, before giving her legs a rest as the tires coasted along the smooth asphalt. She had a better idea.

The road drifted into a shallow curve, the shoulders crumbling away beneath the towering spruce in Salmonberry Bay. The air felt colder on her legs, the sun blocked by the tall trees. An eighteen-wheeler truck roared past her, spraying her shins with gravel. The trailer was piled with logs.

Nicky squeezed the handlebars. How was that possible? Had they already started cutting? They weren't allowed—the vote wasn't finished. They didn't even have a road into the valley.

Anxious, she powered up the short hill. At the top, she heard the faint whine of a saw, and she slowed her bike. From the side of the road she peered through a scrim of alders at logs piled in a mud yard tracked with tire prints. Steam poured from the metal roof of the building behind it, which was open on one side, a network of chains and saws feeding logs into the machinery.

Nicky watched as the eighteen-wheeler snaked its way through the mud, coming to a stop at the open end of the mill. She heard the sigh of the air brakes, then saw a construction vehicle with a prehistoric claw lumber up. The truck driver emerged from his cab and went around the bed, unfastening a series of yellow straps and chains holding down the logs.

She watched as the vehicle advanced, a puff of exhaust emerging from the pipe as the pincers closed. The beep of the vehicle echoed against the mountains as it pushed backwards. Then it lunged forward, depositing the logs onto a platform with a bang and clatter that hurt Nicky's ears. A wave of despair moved over her when she saw spray paint on the cut ends. Under the paint were growth rings, a record of hundreds of winters, some colder than others. All canceled out with the swipe of a saw.

She didn't care what Lars Ruger or Uncle Cliff said. Or that her father was expected to work at the mill. Josie was right. She couldn't just stand there waiting to get struck by lightning. She also knew that yelling at people, making speeches, and holding up signs wasn't something she was good at. She didn't believe it would actually change anyone's mind.

She had resolved that morning, as she opened the curtains to Sky River Valley, to do everything in her power to help them. The trees depended on her. This was her chance.

Loading back onto her bike, she turned at the mill entrance and pointed her front tire downhill. She felt the power and the energy of the trees move through her veins. She started along the mud, picking up speed as she headed toward the screech of the saws.

CHAPTER TWENTY-TWO

Nicky pedaled past the carved wooden head of a man adorned with a blond handlebar moustache and a horned Viking helmet. WELCOME TO THE NORSEMAN MILL the sign beneath it read. She swerved to avoid ruts left by the truck, then skidded the bike to a stop at the main building.

Maybe Josie would announce herself and insist to the person behind the desk that she needed to see the owner. But she wasn't her twin. She wheeled her bike along the side of the building, pausing at a door. Inside she could hear the chug and grind of machinery. Cigarette butts dotted the concrete. She leaned her bike against the metal siding and pulled open the door.

The smell of fresh-cut Christmas trees and the scream of saws greeted her. Blocks of wood that looked like large sticks of butter rattled their way through a chain of tracks and gears. She covered her ears and started scooting along the wall, trying to avoid getting too close to the machinery.

Her boots left prints in the film of sawdust along the concrete.

"Hey, kid! What are you doing?" A heavyset man with a bandanna tied around his throat shot a lever and came toward her. He had a scraggly beard and a lump beneath his bottom lip. He spit into a Styrofoam cup as he approached, then flipped down a plastic shield to cover his face. "C'mon, kid. You shouldn't be on the floor. Don't you got a mask? Where's your hard hat and safety glasses?"

"I want to see Lars," Nicky shouted over the din. "Lars Ruger."

"Lars? Hold up," he said, squinting at her. "Aren't you that kid who spoke the other night at the town hall? Cliff's niece?"

"I'm Nicky Hall, not Josie. I'm her twin sister," she said, holding out one of her curls. "See? No green hair."

"I recognize you. You and your sister have no right telling us our business."

"Is my uncle here?" she asked.

"Yeah, he'll know what to do with you. Follow me. Just don't touch nothing."

He led her along a path that snaked through the equipment. She ducked beneath moving chains, watching as pieces of wood slid along the track above her.

On the other side, the floor opened up, and Nicky could see up to the sheet-metal roof of the building, which was supported by long wooden logs with the bark still attached. Uncle Cliff appeared at the top of a set of metal stairs. "Nicky!" he yelled over the noise. He met her on the stairs, and motioned for her to follow. He held the door to his office open, then shut it behind them. Instantly, the screech went away.

"Hey, love," he said, giving her a quick hug. He smelled like diesel and wood sap. "Is your father here?"

"No. I biked."

"You biked? That's a long trip. What's going on? Is everything okay?"

"I want to talk to Mr. Ruger," she said. "About Sky River Valley."

His eyebrows shot up. "Lars? Oh, I'm pretty sure he's downtown now, trying to get people to vote. Is there something I can help you with?"

Nicky's heart sank. She shifted in her chair and scanned the office, searching for something that might distract her, because she felt like crying. Her eyes landed on a carved swirl of wood, painted red and black. Not unlike the halibut carved into the yellow cedar in the lobby of town hall.

"Is that a whale?" she asked.

"It's a killer whale," Uncle Cliff said. "Orca in English. Kéet in Tlingit. Just like my Tlingit name."

"Did you grow up speaking Tlingit?" Nicky asked.

He reclined in his chair, watching her. "My mother and her brother taught me," he finally said. "She lived in what they called Indian Village in town. They had a government curfew when they were young. They both spoke Tlingit at home. Later they passed it on down." He reached for a metal ball on his desk and rolled it smoothly in one hand.

"Clete said that his grandmother was sent off to a

boarding school in town," Nicky said. "He told me they punished her whenever she didn't speak English."

"That's correct," Uncle Cliff said. "They gave her what
they called an education there. Strangely enough, my mother
went on to become a teacher herself." He set the metal ball
back into its wooden holder. "Listen, Nicky. I'd show you
around a bit, but we're in the midst of cutting a shipment of
wood before the logs from Sky River Valley start arriving. I
wish I had known you were coming so I could have cleared
my schedule."

Nicky's heart thrummed in her ears. "Did town vote to
cut the trees?"

He watched her. "Not yet."

She nodded, turning again to the killer whale carved into
the yellow cedar. "What do you think your grandmother
and her brother would have thought about Sky River Valley?" she said. "I mean, logging it. If they were alive today."

Uncle Cliff's smile vanished. "I think both of them would
have been in favor of anything that would allow me to raise
a family here on this island. That's what I think."

Sweat formed along her brow. Her pulse raced. She
wasn't like Josie. She didn't like picking fights, and making
adults angry. "When I came here today, Uncle Cliff, I just
wanted to tell Lars that this is wrong. I mean, the whole
thing is wrong. I *know* it's the wrong thing."

He shifted in his chair, glancing out the window onto the
mill floor. "And how do you know this, Nicky?"

"I know this sounds crazy, Uncle Cliff. But I can hear
the trees. That night when we came out to your island, it

happened. Except then it was different. I touched a spruce, and it was like stepping behind a waterfall. I touched its bark and—"

"Did Clete take you up into Sky River Valley on Sunday?" he asked. He held her eyes, staring across the desk at her, not moving.

"Yes," she answered.

He watched her coldly. "This ball here on my desk, you know where it's from?"

She shook her head.

"The Russians," he said. "From that man whose statue is outside of town hall. He shelled our island in October of 1804. My ancestors fought back, but the Russians were too strong. They kept firing on Shiskinoow, our fort of saplings, with their fourteen cannons until we had to abandon it. We marched to an island north of here. Then, after some time, we returned to Jackson Cove and built up Indian Village. Did you know that Russian Hill above town had its cannons pointed at Indian Village until 2003, when someone finally decided to point them at the ocean?"

Again, Nicky shook her head.

"I'll tell you one thing my grandmother would never have believed: that Tlingits would be in offices like this, running these machines. That *we* would be the ones making the decisions about our land. We fought hard for this island, and we never gave up. When it was time for us to be patient, we were patient. When it was time to fight, we fought. We fought hard. *No one* tells us what to do."

The power of his voice scared her. He rose and lifted a hard hat from his desk.

"C'mon. Whatever anyone says about you and your sister, or even my own son, you guys have put in your time to understand what's happening in the forest. It's time you understand what's happening in this mill—especially if you're biking all the way out the road, and your daddy's going to work here."

He turned a knob on the back of a hat and handed it to her, along with a set of safety glasses. "Wear these." He opened the door to the scream of machinery, then closed it again. "And these," he said, handing her a plastic package of orange earplugs. "Let's go."

Uncle Cliff led her through the maze of saws and equipment, and out another side door. They reached the far end of the building, where the logs had been deposited. He cupped his hands over his mouth and called something to a worker, then turned back to her.

"Okay. We're about to process these logs. They just came off the barge from Prince of Wales Island, where we've been getting wood for the past couple years, because there's nothing we've been able to cut on Shee. They're going to be rolled into a chute, then chains will feed them into a ring. This here's what we call the primary breakdown, where the trees get made into what we call cants. First order of business is stripping the bark."

Nicky watched as the logs were fed into a circle, which reminded her of a big pencil sharpener. A blur of knives peeled bark from the log.

"From there the headsaw cuts the stick to length. That's the big spinning saw, what we call the Wheel of Fortune, if you kids even watch that show anymore. Slices it like warm butter."

The saw lurched forward. A knot of nausea formed in her stomach as it cut into the thick log. The split pieces wobbled on the track as the metal receded.

"Bingo," Uncle Cliff said. "Once the log's debarked and cut to length, it goes inside. From there, anything can happen, depending on what we type into the computer. We're lucky to have a big mill, and a big floor, so we can change gears easily."

Nicky stood in place, watching a second spruce tree enter the debarker, the whir of blades tearing the skin from the tree. Once more the log advanced, the saw ticking forward, the chains making the sound of a roller coaster chugging uphill. The knot in her stomach loosened as the round blade dove in, the log jerking as it was split to length.

Her uncle ran his fingers over his mouth.

"Do you know that trees can feel pain?" she asked.

"I did not know that," he answered without a smirk.

"It's true," she insisted. "I mean, they don't have nerves like humans. But when a tree is cut it sends a bunch of electrical signals. The cut reacts in the same way wounded human tissue reacts."

"You're telling me these trees are feeling everything that's happening to them?" he asked.

"They're already dead. But when you cut them down, yes."

"Hmm. I guess that would make me an accomplice. Or maybe the perpetrator. A murderer of trees. Then what we're doing here at the mill is butchering."

"Yes," Nicky said, thinking about it.

"C'mon," he said, easing through a door at the end of the building. "Let's go back inside and see the green chain."

"If town votes yes today, when will the trees from Sky River Valley be cut?" Nicky asked.

"We're setting up operations now. If the vote goes our way, and it looks like it will, then we'll start bringing out equipment tomorrow. Set up a tent. Start punching through with a road. Probably get our first logs Wednesday. You know, knock on wood," he said, grinning. "We actually don't want to be cutting before it gets cold, because sap in the trees makes the logs rot quicker."

Nicky's mind raced. Tomorrow, starting at the trailhead where she and Clete first entered the valley, they'd start building a road. *Punching through.*

Clamps gasped as they secured the logs at either end, holding down the trees as a vertical saw rolled forward, lopping off the sides. What had been recognizable as a log before was reduced to a golden bar. The bar was dumped into a chute leading to a pair of twin blades that sliced it into smaller pieces.

"You remember when your dad and I built his guitar shop out back in Danville?" Cliff asked. "That's about what we were using, pieces like that. Then the wood travels to the sanding house, where its edges get smoothed out, and it's ready for packing."

They walked alongside a track lined with slabs of wood moving toward a smaller house. Nicky reached out to touch one. She could still feel the heat in its fibers, and the roughness left by the teeth of the blades.

"That's about that," Uncle Cliff said. "The wood gets put on a pallet and barged down south. People make fences out of it, door jambs, flooring. Homes, and guitar shops, like your dad and I built. Make you any prouder to have your daddy working at the mill?"

Nicky didn't know what to say. It felt like the trip she had taken in elementary school to the pig farm in Elysburg, where she had watched pigs get ushered into a room they wouldn't come out of. She was witnessing what the adults would call a sad but necessary part of life: death.

"Nicky, I know this feels like the end of the world," he said, resting a hand on her shoulder. "But it's not. I promise you. It's not. There are good people working out here, including your father. I know you and your sister are angry because of the valley. But life goes on. We need to live with our decisions and wake up another day to confront the world."

"You sound like my mom," Nicky said as they reached the stairs leading back up to his office.

"That's a great compliment to me," Uncle Cliff said. "Your mother was special, about as great as they come."

Nicky nodded her agreement, and she reached up to hug Uncle Cliff.

"Thanks for the tour," she said.

"Thanks for biking out here," he said. "Hey Nicky," he said as she started toward the stairs.

"What?"

"Don't give up."

She smiled, momentarily confused. Was she telling him to continue to fight?

Before she could say anything, he waved, and shut the door behind him.

Chapter Twenty-Three

Nicky stashed her bike behind the house, and was surprised to find Josie and Clete in the kitchen. He sat in a chair by the table, bathed in sunlight, sipping from a glass of orange juice. Josie looked up when Nicky came in.

"Where have you been?" she asked.

"Out at the mill," Nicky said.

Clete glanced up at her. "Why'd you go out there?"

"Because I wanted to tell Sven's brother that he's making a mistake."

Josie squinted at her. "He was down at the town hall, trying to get people to vote."

"I know. Uncle Cliff was out there. He gave me a tour."

Josie laughed, nodding. "I'll bet that was fun. Maybe he'll give you a chainsaw for Christmas."

"The trees," Clete said. "We lost, Nicky. They're cutting them."

"What?" Nicky sat on the couch across from him.

"The vote," he said. "My mom just told me. Lars is getting

the land. I don't want to be here when this happens. I'll go to school down south with family in Washington. Maybe I'll become a wilderness guide. Or a park ranger, or something. I just can't stay here."

"What about the Three Guardsmen?" Nicky said, her voice rising. "The Old Yellow Cedar? The grove?"

"What are you guys talking about?" Josie snapped. "Is that what you do on your secret expeditions? Come up with fantasy names for trees?"

Clete ignored her. "I don't want to come into town each day, to look up from the harbor and see the valley gone," he said, still addressing Nicky. "To know my father did that. It's too sad."

"Maybe we should climb the trees and not come down," Nicky said, her mind on fire as she thought of solutions. "Or put nails in the trunks, to break the chains of their saws."

Clete shook his head. "None of that works here. The vote is in. It's getting dark earlier. I gotta get back out to the island before sundown."

When he left, Josie continued to stare across the table at Nicky. "I thought I knew you," she said.

"What are you talking about?" Nicky said, rising to pour herself a glass of water.

"It's one thing to stand around, daydreaming or whatever. Actually going to the mill, to the scene of the crime? If you love trees so much, why go watch them get sliced up?"

Nicky drank. She didn't know how to respond.

"What's with you and the trees anyways? You and Clete talk like they're your friends, like you have some special connection. They're just trees. All of this, it's not even about trees, like I told you this morning. It's about the whole earth, and our future."

"No, it's not," Nicky said, standing. "This is about the trees, and this valley. It's about people in Jackson Cove. It's about the island. You wouldn't understand, because lately you can't even take two seconds to walk in someone else's shoes. You're just so . . . selfish."

Josie's nostrils flared. She glared at Nicky, then shook her head. "Sometimes I can't even believe we're twins. I don't even like you anymore." She went down the hall and closed the door to the television room behind her.

PART FIVE

The Old Yellow Cedar

CHAPTER TWENTY-FOUR

That night before dinner Nicky put on her flannel pajamas, climbed over her bed, and scanned the forest. She had heard on the radio that a fall storm was supposed to blow in, but the sky remained clear, though the temperature had dropped.

Their father had a frozen pizza in the oven, and he called up to the girls that it was ready. When they came down he was nowhere to be seen. Josie ate a piece at the table without bothering to pick off the pepperoni. Nicky took her slice back up to the attic. She finished her crust, then thought about going back downstairs to brush her teeth, but decided instead to crawl into her bed and pull the covers over her head. She heard her sister come upstairs, the floorboards creaking as she crossed the room. She waited for her to say something. But a few minutes later, she was asleep.

No sooner had Nicky closed her eyes than she awoke to a whine. At first she thought it was a mosquito pestering her. But there were no mosquitoes in Jackson Cove, she remembered Clete saying. Then she thought it was the storm people were predicting.

She sat up. The moon shined through Josie's window, covering her sister's body in gray light, illuminating the painted floorboards. Nicky turned and opened her window. The tips of the trees in the valley reflected the cool white light. She let her eyes lazily run toward the back of the valley, as if flying over the forest. She saw the Old Yellow Cedar, high above the rest, reassuring in its stature. Then the whine became louder, evening out, echoing between the mountains. The branches of the cedar began to shake. She heard a crack, followed by a whoosh and clatter. Then the valley settled, and resumed its silence.

Nicky pulled the window open farther, gripping the sill and leaning out, still not believing the information her eyes had conveyed. Had anyone else heard that? She looked to either side of her. No lights.

What she had just seen didn't make sense. Just a hole remained where the cedar had been, as if someone had put a drain in the valley floor to empty it of moonlight.

Nicky's heart slammed in her chest as she rose from her bed and pulled on cargo pants. She tiptoed past her father's door, padded down the stairs, stepped into her XtraTufs, and shut the front door behind her. She took the bike from the shed and stumbled as she dragged it into the road. It had been a dream. It had to have been a dream. It just wasn't possible.

"Where you off to in such a rush, sailor?"

She froze with one foot on a pedal. Off to the left, Sven's

cigarette glowed. At his feet Rooster lapped milk from a silver dish. Sven smashed his cigarette into the boardwalk and
dropped the butt into a rusted coffee can.

"You got an important date at this late hour, with a storm
coming in?" Her foot hovered over the pedal. She couldn't
find words. "Your face is about as pale as that moon up there,
and it won't be out for long, the way the wind's blowing.
What's got you so worked up?"

"I just—I need to check on something."

"Sailor, do you recall that evening on the ferry when we
first met? Pulling away from Bellingham? You were sadder
than a baby who lost her rattle."

"I remember," she said.

"You looked at me like nothing in the world would ever
change again. Like there were no answers to your problems."

"I remember," she repeated, growing impatient.

"Look at you now. It's three in the morning, and you're
about to go into the Alaska woods with a fall storm blowing
in. Where did such courage come from?"

"I don't know," she said honestly.

"Nicky, you take that bike and you go check on what you
need to check on. Rooster and I, we'll be waiting for you.
Take care when it starts blowing sideways."

When Sven said this, Rooster glanced up from her pan
of milk, fixing her golden eyes on Nicky just as she had
that first evening on the ferry. Nicky gave a quick nod, then
pushed down on her pedals, starting down the hill toward
the harbor. As she biked she scanned for a kayak—she could
paddle to Clete's house, wake him, and they could go out

together to see what had happened. Then she saw his skiff tied up at the loading dock, the blue canvas cover and spray skirt bobbing in the growing waves. Uncle Cliff must have slept at the mill, she figured, probably worried about skiffing into town with the storm.

She turned her bike around and started along the road in the direction of Sky River Valley, ignoring the chill against her cheeks. Nicky flipped up her hood, then thought about returning for gloves, and maybe an extra layer for the storm. She could be quiet enough not to wake her father, or Josie. Then she thought of the hole in the valley, and the Old Yellow Cedar toppled along the forest floor.

Courage, she thought. The forest needed her. Now.

CHAPTER TWENTY-FIVE

She passed the trooper academy, the parking lot flooded with white light, and started down Sky River Road. Backhoes and smaller vehicles sat at rest, their claws folded, asleep on pillows of gravel. Orange cones gleamed in the moonlight, set out around the machines. Farther along, Josie made out the dark shape of the big pincer machine from the mill. Up close its rubber tires were just as large as the Wheel of Fortune blade, twice as tall as her. Its steel claws reflected the moonlight, then went dark as a shield of clouds blew over. As she neared the trailhead, a heavier wind charged through the trees, lifting and dropping the branches.

A drab green tent had been set up at the trailhead. The fabric glinted in the moonlight. Nicky leaned her bike against a rock and peeked inside, where she saw a collection of pallets covered in blue tarps. She lifted the corner of a tarp. Steel wires looped in piles sat alongside ten or so new chainsaws in orange plastic cases. She smelled sweet gas, and picked out plastic cherry-red cans in the dark, alongside gallon jugs of chainsaw lubricant.

She walked the maze of pallets toward the trail, resisting the urge to take up the cherry cans and dump gas on everything, setting it afire. Instead, she switched on her headlamp. The white light lit up the dappled dark of a nearby Sitka spruce.

Sven was right. On that ferry she had been so sad and alone. Now, she decided, she was someone different. Unafraid of this silvery, rich wind that brought these fall storms to the island, perfect for toppling trees without deep roots. Unafraid of these machines, lined up like an army about to assault.

Taking a deep breath, she started into the woods.

Once beneath the canopy, despite the winds along Sky River Road, the world hushed. Thickets of fog drifted between the boughs. The moon returned, filtering in shards of tinsel-colored light through the branches, making jagged shapes in the moss. Somewhere behind her a branch crackled. It sounded like a firecracker, and she froze, pivoting her head to shine the headlamp into the woods. After a moment she reached up to switch it off. It felt safer to be moving through the forest without being lit up.

It wasn't Uncle Cliff, Nicky decided as she stepped over the roots and picked her way along the trail, listening for the wind, which sounded like a far-off freight train. It must be Lars. She could even picture him there, removing his tortoiseshell glasses, lowering the chainsaw into the cedar, gritting his chipped yellow teeth as the blades spit plumes of sawdust. Wanting to be the first to draw blood against the forest, and his father, by toppling the oldest, tallest tree in the valley.

She quickened her pace. New chanterelles, no larger than her thumb, poked their caramel heads up from the moss. She touched one, then pulled her hand back to quiet the screams that instantly filled her. The forest was in pain. The leader of the family was gone.

She started to jog along the trail. Then she ran.

As she made her way up the valley, the trees seemed to greet her with hisses of needles. She had failed them. This was her fault. The sky clouded over again, though the moon still cast a wan light upon the moss and downed trees. Each time she dropped back into a walk, out of breath, the hiss of trees grew louder. Could Lars not even wait for first light? Had he been dreaming for so long, perhaps even as a child growing up with Sven, of cutting that tree? Of course he had to take the king of the forest. Then she was running again.

She neared the second bridge, and smelled a musty scent. She slowed her pace, and felt her ears come alive to some new danger. The smell of wet moss and old meat and something chemical. The smell of hospitals and school halls in the morning. Of seagull guano on the breakwater rocks, and on the ferry. Ammonia.

Then, just off the right side of the trail, the salmonberry bushes parted, and a shape rose. At first she thought that the storm had caught her, and that these fall winds she had heard so much about were now revealing a particular spot where a sapling was taking life before her very eyes, like some giant beanstalk. Then the monstrous, bullet-shaped head turned to her, and the jaws opened and closed, revealing a slash of teeth. The pungent smell swirled around her, causing a gripping in her stomach. She ached to run, but remembered Clete.

Don't say the name, she remembered. *Don't even* think *the name.*

The roar of the creature sent an impulse of such acute fright right down her spine that she lost feeling in her legs. The salmonberries quaked all around the dark shape. She ached to be somewhere else, anywhere else. After a moment, she was still in place, facing the apparition, which appeared both exquisite, otherworldly, and awful.

She kept her eyes on the trail, and began to slowly back away. "Hello," she said, trying to remember what Clete had told her to do, but only coming up with the tune *Row row row your boat.* "I don't mean any harm. I'm just passing through. This is your home, not mine. I'll go away soon, I promise."

As she spoke these words, Nicky focused on the tips of her boots, observing where the tan band around the sole met the darker brown. A heavy gust moved through the branches, signaling the storm's arrival. The trees wailed as the branches shook side to side, the trunks wobbling all around her. She heard a snarfing, followed by a shuffling. When she looked up again, the shape was gone, just a whiff of old meat remaining.

218

She gathered herself, pausing to close her eyes and offer thanks to the forest, and to the world around her. Squaring her shoulders toward the head of the valley, she continued deeper into the woods.

At the second bridge, she forced herself to slow. She took the stump stairs one by one, holding the railing as she walked the length of the cedar to protect against the wind running up the river. The sky above had turned a milky purple. A few fish splashed below, their white bellies flashing. She caught her dim reflection in the running water, then made her hands into fists and covered her eyes, allowing herself to slip into blackness and pretend, for a moment, that she wasn't in a forest full of bears, about to walk off-trail into a valley as a storm threatened.

When she opened her eyes, the river still ran. She looked up it, hoping to see her mother standing in the water, encouraging her to press on and be brave. But there was only the water curling around the rocks, slipping beneath the tree boughs waving in the wind.

On the other side of the bridge she dropped down from the log and began running again, this time smelling the air, ready for another encounter. The trail curved away from the river. Her eyes ran along the devil's club, whose leaves had turned yellow with cold. She didn't even slow at the opening, just plunged through, ignoring the scrapes on her cheeks, the needles jabbing at her scalp, digging into the side of her neck. She cleared the leaves and felt the flatness of the game trail beneath her boots. Ducking hemlock branches, she accelerated again. As she approached the grove, the trees came alive, the trunks wobbling in the wind and the needles making a sheering sound. A gentle rain worked through the branches. Her cheeks were moist with rainwater, and something else. Blood, she saw, looking down at her fingers. From the thorns of the devil's club.

The band of light was coming up over the mountains as her boots sank into the spongey soil of the first muskeg. She could feel the earth beneath her crackling, as if the entire expanse had been shot through with current. Along the fringes the trees seemed to sparkle with energy. Even the moss was alive. She brushed her cheek against her shoulder to clean off the blood and kept going.

On the far side she pushed through the thicket of alders, climbing the hedgerow to the second muskeg. She watched as a pearl of dew caught in the filaments of old-man's beard shined in the early morning light, then vanished in a howl of wind. The earth swayed beneath her feet as she ran past cloudy brown ponds, the surfaces sloshing. Sorrow began to work into her muscles. She didn't know if the trees were spreading it through her, from the earth, if it was the electricity or magnetism of the incoming storm, or her own sadness, accumulated over the past year, breaking like a wave over her.

She should have been out here, storm or not. In the forest. Protecting the trees. They had asked her. They had depended on her. Instead, she had fought with her sister, and fallen asleep in her attic. She had been selfish, so selfish, caught up in her own sadness. And now she was paying for it.

Closing her eyes, holding her hands to her face to protect from thorns, she pushed through the brush separating the last muskeg from the grove. The fear she had felt from her encounter on the trail slid into anger. "Lars!" she yelled, her fingers itching as she cleared the branches. She felt the urge to tear him apart. His pride and his smirk and his selfishness. All Josie's righteous anger at adults filled her as she muscled through the last barrier of devil's club. She didn't even register the scrape of the thorns on her forehead and cheeks and the backs of her hands.

As she broke through to the other side, the first thing she noticed was the bruised sky where the cedar had once been, just an inky welt filled in with clouds. The Three Guardsmen seemed to be leaning in, hovering over the downed tree, which stretched across the forest floor, branches of smaller trees sticking out, crushed beneath its bulk.

Then she saw him. Sitting atop the cedar, directly over the stream. He had undone his bun, and his wet hair covered his face as his shoulders heaved. He was cross-legged, crying into his hands. With the wind she could hear nothing, but at the base of the trunk Nicky saw the chainsaw, small and powerless, like a pin beside a deflated balloon.

She balanced on a moss-covered branch, and climbed to the main trunk, gripping the wet, soft green where the bough grew steep. She pulled herself up, reached the avenue of bark that stretched as far as she could see.

"Clete!" she yelled. Her boots sank into the mossy trunk.

It extended so far ahead of her that the idea of reaching the top made her dizzy. Leaning into the wind and soft rain, she forced herself forward.

"I had to. I had to," Clete chanted over the wind when she reached him. "It was the only way for people to see."

She stood over her cousin and started to cry. "Why?"

"Nicky," Clete cried, turning around and standing, "I cut the cedar down, just like the trees asked." His eyes were swollen, his cheeks soaked in tears. A gust nearly pushed them off the trunk, and they both crouched along the bark.

"I knew you'd come," Clete said as he started to control his weeping. "The trees said you'd hear. I wasn't sure you'd have the courage. But you're here."

"I saw it from my window. I heard it."

"You're bleeding. You've got blood all over, and you look pale. You're not dressed for this weather. It's only going to get worse," he said as a gust howled through the forest.

"I saw one," she said simply. "I saw a—you know. On the trail. Then the storm started, and I think he got scared."

"Did he charge?" Clete asked, suddenly paying close attention to her.

She shook her head. "I looked down, like you told me. I noticed everything around me. I was patient."

Clete nodded. "The forest, even the animals—they know death is coming. They just want to breathe. It's going to be a bloodbath. This cedar—it's just the beginning. This stream, it will get filled in with branches and bark. The salmon will stop coming. The hemlocks, the cedar, and the spruce—even the alders. All of them destroyed, gone. The muskeg will be drained and filled in with cement to make a parking lot. We won't recognize this land."

"There's something," Nicky insisted as she recalled her father describing the tune he couldn't quite hear. "There's something we're not seeing."

"There's nothing," Clete said over the wind as he started down the cedar. "Except to get out of these woods before this storm really blows through. A tree could fall on us."

"You mean, the wind could push one over."

"Yes," he said. "The bedrock is shallow, and the trees have no good taproot. They come down in storms like this."

"Have the trees given up?" Nicky asked as she followed him down. "Have you heard them since you cut the cedar?"

Clete shook his head.

Nicky picked an alternate route, lowered herself through the branches to the soil. As she crossed the moss, she thought of her mother chanting when she couldn't figure something out. *Problem, solution. Problem, solution.*

She stopped at the base of one of the hemlock Guardsmen. Clete sat in the branches of the cedar, watching. She wrapped her arms around the tree. She could feel her heart beating hard against the bark, as if nothing—no ribs, no flesh—separated her.

Then, taking a deep breath, she leaned over and clutched a mushroom.

She expected to hear screams, as she had earlier that morning on the way out. Only sorrow moved through her, a slicing, bitter sound, mimicking the winds of the storm blowing off the ocean. Then something else, that brought her back to the skiff ride out with Uncle Cliff. A dizzying, immense sadness, punctuated by bolts of unease.

Nicky pulled back her hand. She looked at Clete, who had come down off the trunk and stood now beside her.

"It's not working," she said. "I just feel sick."

"Try these," Clete said, pointing to another group of mushrooms, growing from the great wheel of the cedar stump. "The roots, they must have all this energy to send up with no branches left above ground. Whatever it is, it's going to be loud."

She squinted against the driving rain and leaned forward to touch the largest of the mushrooms, ignoring the roiling of her stomach. Immediately she felt a bright pulse of energy move through her arm. Clete called to her, but she couldn't make out his words. His face appeared panicked, but she couldn't tear herself away from the teeming nest of sorrow, insistent and loud, filling her ears. It was the thinnest thread of a tune, so faint she could hardly hear it.

She looked up into the slanted branches of a Guardsman, which rose into the night sky like a pillar. She turned her gaze back to the jagged base of the cedar, where Clete had hacked with his chainsaw, closing her eyes and reaching, with her other hand, for another mushroom, doing her best to concentrate as the sound grew louder, resolving into an eerie electric chant.

Look around.

She opened her eyes. One by one, windblown trees across

the grove began to light up, blinking like fireflies. Slowly, she turned to Clete, who looked out over the forest as the toppled trees glowed with an unearthly phosphorescence. Trees caught in diagonals, or resting in hills of moss, releasing a rhythmic beat as they pulsed.

Then she knew. The answer was music.

CHAPTER TWENTY-SIX

She let go of the mushrooms and focused on Clete, who stood before her with his hands gripping her raincoat. "What did you hear?" he asked.

She broke away, and picked up his chainsaw. "Is there still gas in this? Can you use it to take the bark off a tree?" she asked.

"What?"

"Come here."

"Nicky, this wind and rain is only going to get worse. We need to get out of the forest. And I need to tell my father what I did. He'll be furious."

She took the chainsaw over to one of the logs she had seen glow. "Just take off the top layer."

"Why?" he repeated.

"Just, please."

Clete pulled the cord on the chainsaw, which snarled back at him, coughing smoke. He lowered the saw into the damp, moss-heavy bark, taking off a strip. Bright blond wood shined so hard it hurt her eyes. She tapped it with her knuckles. Hard and smooth.

"Instruments," she shouted to him. "These trees, they're instruments." Clete just stared back at her, his idling chainsaw in one hand.

"We need to get back to town and tell Josie and Veronica."

"Tell them what?" Clete said, confused.

Nicky climbed the log, slick with rain, to cross the river. Just a faint print remained in the sand. The river below didn't frighten her at all. "We need to tell them that the mill can be kept in business without cutting down the valley. That there's a better answer."

"Lars will never let that happen," Clete said, following behind with his chainsaw. "I doubt my dad will either."

"C'mon," Nicky said, pushing through the bushes. "We only have until daylight."

PART SIX

The Plan

CHAPTER TWENTY-SEVEN

B y the time they reached the harbor the wind had settled, and the sky had started to clear. The temperature had dropped, and a skim of frost covered the dock
planks. Nicky's breath pushed out in front of her as they
powered up the hill to the house.

"You two look like dogs caught out in the rain. Good
luck that williwaw wasn't worse."

Nicky turned to Sven, who was sitting on his wooden
stoop, sipping coffee. Rooster slept in a tangle of blankets
beside him, her black fur rising and falling.

"We got caught out in the valley," Clete said.

"Kissing goodbye to the trees, one by one?" Sven said,
giving them a silvery smile that matched the dawn sky.
"Looks like you locked horns with a needle-beast, sailor,"
Sven said to Nicky. "Good thing a bear didn't scent you with
all that dried blood. What's the plan now?"

"We've got a new plan," Nicky said.

Sven nodded toward a canvas backpack stained with

black grease. "I followed you out there, sailor, just to be sure you didn't get blown off your bike. You seemed to have a handle on things, and I got bored, so I decided I'd relieve those loggers of their chains. It'll buy you a few hours to get your plan in place, but I don't suggest you stand around here much longer. Best go make it happen. Do it for your kids. And your kids' kids."

Nicky met the old man's gaze. "Thanks, Sven."

"You got it. Now go!"

They ran up the stairs into the apartment, passing her father's bedroom, and went up into the attic. The floors were bright with the scrubbed morning sun.

"Josie!" Nicky called as she crawled over her sister's bed. "Wake up."

Josie sprung up from the pillows. "What did I tell you about coming up here!" she yelled, her eyes blazing at Clete. "This is not your room!"

"We just got back from Sky River Valley," Nicky said breathlessly. "We have a plan to stop them from cutting the trees. But we need your help."

Josie flung off the covers and stomped across the room in her sweatpants, unplugging her phone from its charger and checking it. "Are you two crazy? Neither of you lifted a finger when people were voting. All of a sudden you have some master plan. Let me give you some advice. Go back to what you were doing, being fairies in the woods or whatever it was, and leave the rest of us to deal with reality."

Nicky crossed the room and snatched the phone from

her sister's hands. "Call Veronica. Now. And her father. He can make a Facebook page. A website. We need to use it to invite the widest community possible. Now."

"What has gotten into you?" Josie said. "You need to settle down. Veronica? First off, it's seven-thirty in the morning. She's sleeping, like any normal person would be in this cold weather."

"Wake them up!" Nicky screamed. Josie froze, and her eyes went wide. "Wake them up," Nicky repeated, this time without shouting. "Tell Veronica to come here with her father in thirty minutes."

"Who *are* you?" Josie said as she took her phone back. "You can't just *build* a website."

"We can announce and advertise what we're doing with a front page."

"And what are we doing?" Josie said.

Nicky stepped toward her sister. "I will tell you, but you need to help us right now, or get out of the way. We need to alert people all over the world about the clearcut. No one understands there's a rainforest in Alaska—and especially not one in danger. No one knows that trees over a thousand years old are about to be destroyed. There are people who care, but their caring is worth nothing if others on the ground can't report on it. Can't bear witness. So. Are you in?"

Josie looked over at Clete, as if he might tell her that what she just heard was crazy. Instead, he shrugged and said, "She's got a plan. And I'm with her."

Josie turned back to Nicky, who took her shoulders and pleaded with her eyes. "Remember? Problem, solution. Problem, solution. All we can do is try."

"Fine," Josie finally said, reaching for her vest. "I don't care anymore. No one on this island seems to like me anyways, so why not go down in flames."

"Great. So you'll call?" Nicky said.

"I'll call. Veronica's father, Nathan Deschumel, has a huge group of followers on Jackson Cove Convos. That's probably the best place to start. First we need to convince this community that your plan holds water."

"Tell them to be here in half an hour. In our kitchen."

"Why not this second?" Josie asked, zipping up her vest and swiping open her phone.

Nicky glanced down the stairs. "Because first, we need to convince our own father."

A few minutes later Josie and Nicky sat at the kitchen table, listening to coffee percolate.

"It's a cool idea, but it's just not going to fly," Dad said. "It's just not feasible."

"Don't shut this out, please," Nicky said. "It's the same as what you and Uncle Cliff did with your shop. Just on a much bigger scale."

Their father rubbed his bloodshot eyes, then blinked a few times to clear sand from his lashes. "Nicky, I appreciate your sudden energy. We're talking about a whole different set of skills and tools. A whole different set of financial realities. You can't just snap your fingers and teach people to build a soundboard. Or retool an entire mill, for that matter. It's just not possible."

"But Nicky's right. The wood is Sitka spruce," Josie said. "You yourself told us, it's what musicians all over the world use for instruments. This forest—the Tongass—it's where your soundboards come from, right?"

"Yes, that's right," he admitted. "For tone wood you can't beat it. If you're making a guitar, you generally make it out of Sitka spruce."

"Exactly. Dad, why not build the instruments right here on the island. It's foolish to ship the wood off, especially seeing as how everyone needs jobs."

"That still means you're cutting trees down," he said. "Maybe not as many, but you're cutting them just the same."

"No," Nicky said. "That's the thing. The trees are already down."

"We're only using salvage, Uncle Danny," Clete explained. "The ones that have already fallen. Most of the trees come down in the fall, because that's when the winds come through. The wood is still good because the sugary sap doesn't rot them. That's why my dad wants to cut the whole valley in the next few months."

Their father stood up, looking between Nicky and Josie. "Okay, I get it," he finally said. "I see what you're trying to do, which is take the role of your mother, and give me a guitar shop. I wish I could have that, and that everything could go back to the way it was. You two are the sweetest—and you too, Clete. It makes me so happy to see you three cousins working together, as a family. But life just doesn't work that way. There are forces on this island we can't control. That goes for you too, Clete. Saving this forest isn't going to change the past, or get you out of any future that you're trying to avoid."

His condescending tone riled her. She tried to push back her anger, and then recalled how her mother often convinced her dad when he said no, by overwhelming him with facts.

"The cutting has already started," she said. "Clete brought down the Old Yellow Cedar this morning."

His eyes went wide behind his glasses. "Clete did *what?*"

"I chopped it down," Clete admitted. "This morning. I wanted to show everyone how awful it was."

"I don't understand. There's no way you could have done that alone."

Clete shrugged. "That tree isn't standing anymore?" he said, turning toward the window.

"You can't even see the valley from there," Nicky said as he craned his neck to see past Sven's roof. "Dad, the other day I biked out to the mill. Uncle Cliff gave me a tour. Then this morning I woke up to the sound of a chainsaw. Out my window I saw the Old Yellow Cedar fall. I walked into the valley, and I could feel it. I could feel them. I can *hear* them."

"Who is 'them'?" he snapped. "You're telling me you were out there this morning? In the forest? I don't understand any of this, and I'm starting to get frustrated."

"The trees," she answered calmly. "I know this sounds crazy, but they protected me. I can tap into them. Their network. I don't know why, but I can. This morning they showed me something clearly. I felt it. All over. I need you to talk to Lars Ruger and Uncle Cliff. You need to tell them to come here. In half an hour, and we can all work out a plan."

He started laughing. "A plan? What, that my magical daughter wants to sabotage their jobs—come listen to her ideas? I'm supposed to be selling this wood that they're cutting. Not stopping them before they even get started."

"Fine," Josie broke in, looking at her sister, then at her dad. "Don't tell them about the plan. Just tell them they can make more money in the woods by building instruments, instead of clearcutting the forest. They'll also make more friends."

"By using trees that have already fallen," he said, with a tone of sarcasm.

"Exactly," Josie said. "You need to convince them of all that. You owe us that."

"I owe you?"

"Yes. Tell them a guitar factory will create more jobs than a traditional wood mill. They want to make money— tell them a guitar factory will make more money. Clete and Nicky say there are over a hundred downed Sitka spruce trees out there. That could keep folks on the island busy at a factory for ten years, bringing in three times what a conventional mill would. It's called value-adding. You're taking the wood and —"

"I know what 'value-adding' means, Josie." He shook his head. "I'm not going to call them. That's final."

Nicky glanced at the wall clock. She heard a knock.

"That's Veronica and Nathan," Josie said, starting down

the stairs. Her father's resistance seemed to have boosted her energy. "I'm going to work with them in the television room to get everything ready."

"Got it," Nicky said.

"What are they doing here?" their father asked.

"Helping us," Josie said as she left the kitchen and went down the stairs.

Her father took off his glasses. "I was worried about your sister, and now I'm worried about you, Nick. Your attachment to this valley—it's good. I like that you care. But we don't have any power. I wish I had a better way to tell you. But things don't happen like this."

"Dad," Nicky said, as she picked his phone up from the kitchen table. "Please, call. Try."

"I'm working for these guys, kiddo. I can't just tell them to show up at my house on a Monday morning."

"I just texted my dad," Clete said, holding up his phone. "I told him I cut down the cedar. He'll be here in fifteen minutes."

"He's coming?" their father said.

Clete nodded.

"This is getting out of control. Okay. Give me that phone. I'll call Lars."

CHAPTER TWENTY-EIGHT

At just after nine a.m. that Monday, Veronica, Nathan, Lars, Uncle Cliff, Josie and Nicky, Clete, and Danny spread out around the kitchen, all of them wearing masks. Nathan sat at the kitchen table typing on his laptop, his silver hair sparkling in the morning light. Lars stood by the door, blinking behind his tortoiseshell glasses and glancing at his phone. "I've got about five minutes," he announced. "Someone trickster stole the chains off our saws, and I'm having to GoldStreak some in from Juneau."

Nicky tried not to smile as she stood to address them. "You know I am Nicky Hall," she began. "You probably recognize me because you've seen my sister. Except I don't have green hair." No one laughed. She took a breath, and continued.

"I know this is strange, but what I ask of you this morning is just that you listen. To Clete. To me, and Josie, and Veronica. We know the vote to cut Sky River Valley passed yesterday. We know that equipment is gathered at the trail-head. But we have a new proposition."

"I just want to say, if I can," Lars interrupted, pulling down his mask, "that I—that we, at the Norseman Mill—appreciate the involvement of the young people in this whole process. We want to be a friend to you. How do you call it, Nathan?" he said, looking at Veronica's father. "An ally? I—we—want to be an ally. So we are listening."

"Thank you, Mr. Ruger," Nicky said, stopping him. "As we speak, Mr. Deschumel is working on a website called Sky River Valley Instruments."

Nathan turned his laptop around so everyone could see the screen. "That's right. I've already purchased the domain name. SkyRiverAlaska.com. Here's our landing page."

They all leaned in to examine the photo of the mossy rainforest, and the words "Sustainably built instruments from salvaged Alaska Sitka spruce. Produced on Shee Island."

Lars nodded slowly. "Interesting. I like this, Nathan. Congratulations. I thought you had retired. You're looking for investors, I assume? I could set up some meetings in Seattle."

Uncle Cliff readjusted his baseball hat. He kept giving disbelieving stares at Clete, who sat in his customary corner of the couch.

"We have a post up on Jackson Cove Convos," Josie said, standing beside Nicky. "So far, there have been over a thousand likes, and 258—no, 260—comments," she said, looking at her phone.

"That's wonderful!" Lars said. "New businesses are exactly what Jackson Cove needs."

Josie stared back at him, unblinking. "You should be congratulating yourself, Mr. Ruger. Because it's your new business."

The man pursed his thin lips and cocked his head. "Beg pardon? I don't follow."

"That's because you keep interrupting," Josie said.

Nicky started again. "Our plan is to convert the Norseman Mill to instrument fabrication. The Wheel of Fortune, and the other front-end saws would remain. On the back end, you would build instruments. It could employ three times as many people. Training the workers won't cost that much. It would require less wood—significantly less—but make more money."

Lars's jaw dropped, as if he was about to speak. He continued to stare at Josie, then began peering around the room, as if searching for an explanation.

"I said the other night that we should just leave the forest alone," Josie said. "But Clete and my sister have convinced Veronica and me that it's reasonable to use salvaged wood to build guitars and other instruments. Mandolins. Violins. Maybe even an ancient lyre. Or a Russian balalaika. That could be cool."

Their father sat beside Clete on the couch, shaking his head. "There's just no way, girls."

"No," Lars began, his voice gathering momentum. "No, there's not. I agree. As I said, thank you for this interest in my affairs. You frankly have no right to post like that on the community website. No right indeed. Nathan, I'm surprised you let this fly. In fact, I'm well within my rights to call my lawyers and press charges."

"I helped with the posts," Nathan said. "Anything that happens, you can blame it on me, Lars. As you know, I've made my living investing in start-ups. This is an excellent idea. In fact, I just shot off a text to EcoTrust in Portland, to one of my program officers there. He got back immediately and said he he'd like to know more. I have investor friends not only in Seattle, but also in Silicon Valley. Instead of cutting down rainforest, we make guitars from it. It's simple. Concise. No one wants another clearcut. Especially not trees that have been growing for a thousand years."

Lars started to pace. "I don't understand any of this. This is *my* mill. *My* company. Town just voted to allow me to cut these trees. At this point, no one can tell me what to do."

"Mr. Ruger," Nicky said, surprised by the calm tone of her voice. "We're not telling you what to do. We're suggesting a way for you to make more money. Can we start by agreeing that we would all rather have the products be manufactured here, instead of the wood just cut up and shipped to China, or to the Lower 48?"

"Well," Lars said, glancing at Uncle Cliff, "in an ideal world. But we don't *live* in an ideal world."

"That's the thing," Nicky said, her voice warming. "Those Sitka spruce logs, they're out there waiting for us. It *is* an ideal situation. Clete and I cut into one this morning.

242

The wood is pristine. Don't you see? This is a chance to save this valley and not devastate the community. To *help* it."

"Our mill is built to process individual lumber," Uncle Cliff said. "We sell raw material. It's what we do. We get wood from the woods, and we cut it. It's *that* simple."

"You're still going to get the wood from the woods, Dad," Clete said. "We can still use all the equipment. We just get to add the manufacturing, so the profits are greater locally."

When Cliff didn't respond, Nicky turned to him and pressed the point. "Remember when you told me yesterday that the Norseman is built for primary preparation?" Nicky said. "You told me how the 'green chain' saws trees into cants. That's exactly what my dad uses for his guitar tops."

"How do you know all this?" Lars asked.

"Because I showed her the mill," Uncle Cliff said, sighing.

"And what do you mean 'your tops'?" Lars growled, turning to their father.

"Back in Danville I had my own shop," their father explained. "Behind my house. I made instruments. Mostly guitars. Resonators. A few mandolins."

"He's the best," Josie said, beaming at her father. "Everyone wanted one of his guitars. There were waiting lists. He's also great with people, which I know is why you hired him," she said, turning back to Lars.

"It could be the first guitar shop in Alaska," Veronica added.

"Clete and I calculated that, given that you won't have any shipping costs, since the wood is already on the island, you only need one hundred salvaged Sitka spruce from the forest for the mill to produce about twenty thousand guitar tops a year," Nicky said. "Depending on the final cost of the guitar, that will make you twice as much as what you're making now. I have all the numbers. All the wood is *right here*, on the island."

"Out of rotting trees?" Lars said incredulously.

"Mr. Ruger," Clete said. "Nicky and I can show you downed Sitka spruce logs right around the Old Yellow Cedar that could be used for building guitars. They're all just waiting, with clean wood beneath the bark, like Nicky said. We checked one this morning. The wood still has integrity."

Lars raked his fingers through his blond-and-pewter hair. "This is preposterous." He stared down at Cliff, who stood with his legs crossed, leaning against a counter.

"It would be a huge retooling," Uncle Cliff said. "You'd need some fine-toothed band saws."

"A kiln," their father added.

"We have the kiln," Uncle Cliff said. "The boy's right. It's the sun that's rough on dead fiber. Especially in the grove there, with those old trees. Only about three percent of light gets to the forest floor. When a tree blows down, that wood stays hard as a nut. All that salvage out there is probably still good."

"It is," Nicky insisted. "We saw it."

"Cliff, are you serious? You're actually considering this?" Lars said. "We'd have to helicopter out the logs. Even if we *bought* a helicopter, it would be too expensive to retrofit the shop. Two million dollars, at least."

"We wouldn't even have to helicopter them out," Cliff said. "We could work back there to break them down, then four-wheel the logs. Use the Alaskan mill. The kids are right. All the blowdown in that valley would be enough to keep us in business for ten years or more. Better than straight logging, anyway."

"Imagine," Veronica said, stepping forward and standing beneath the overhead light, delivering her winning smile. "Yo-Yo Ma sitting down to a cello from salvaged wood from our forest. Would you rather have that?" Her voice dropped, turning sinister. "Or a bunch of small-town middle-schoolers putting it all over social media how the heart of a thousand-year-old yellow cedar is being used to build fences in Somewhere, USA. Think about that."

Lars met eyes with Veronica's father, who stared right back at him. "Is your teenage daughter trying to extort me, Nathan?"

Nathan put up his hands. "She calls it as she sees it, Lars. I have no control over her."

Lars turned to Nicky. "I've let you make your argument. But we're cutting down those trees. All of them." His coffee sloshed as he set it down on the counter and started for the door. "And you," he said, pointing at Nicky's father, "I suggest you load back into your camper, or whatever that thing is, and find another island for your girls to make trouble on. You're out of a job."

"Don't talk to my daughters like that," their father said, straightening and following Lars out of the kitchen. "Go on. Get out of my house."

"You're a renter, buddy. Get off my island," Lars shouted as the heels of his loafers fell heavy on the wood steps. The door slammed behind him.

When their father came back into the kitchen, Josie smiled. "At least it's not me doing it this time."

After a moment, he started to laugh, giving a soft, disbelieving shake of the head.

"You four," Cliff said, looking at them all and smiling. "A bunch of troublemakers."

"We created trouble," Clete said, who still had cedar shavings stuck to his fuzzy wool sweater.. "But I don't think we got anywhere."

"I guess that means we go to Plan B," Nicky said.

Clete looped an elastic into his hair. Nathan slapped the tabletop with his palms. "I love Plan B," he said. "I don't think it's got a chance, but something tells me we should try. Now is someone going to tell me exactly what is Plan B?" he asked, looking around the room.

"Yes," Cliff echoed. "What is Plan B?"

"Why should we tell you?" Josie said. "You're the enemy."

Uncle Cliff watched his niece, his eyes going cold, then soft again. "I'm your family, kid."

Their father glanced at his phone and opened the case for his guitar. "Plan B is already in action. Mall is waiting for us at the trailhead. So is Alice. C'mon, Cliff."

"To do what?" he asked, pushing himself off the counter.

"To go into the valley," Nicky said. "And make some noise."

PART SEVEN

Sharing the Forest

CHAPTER TWENTY-NINE

A few ravens hopped along the trunk of the Old Yellow Cedar as the four kids and five adults pushed through the devil's club into the grove of old growth.

"My goodness, son," Aunt Mall said, lifting her camera and snapping a photo. "You slayed a wooly mammoth. I can't even fit the tree into my frame." She strode over the moss, trying to get a good angle.

Uncle Cliff ran a calloused hand over the bark. "How'd you topple this beast without getting it hung up?"

"I've watched you enough times," Clete said. He scampered up a branch and stood on the trunk, the ravens hopping out of his way, but not flying off.

"Nicky, do you think your dad should play up there? Or in front of the tree?" Nathan asked as he set up a tripod.

"In front," Alice answered for her. "Gives a sense of the girth of the cedar. It's hard for people off the island to appreciate. This is going around the world, right?"

"Absolutely," Nathan said. "Also into the *Jackson Cove Courier*. Right, Mallory?"

"Oh yeah," Aunt Mall said, lifting her notebook and giving it a shake. "I'm getting it all down."

"Dad, when we go live, can you put a banner up? Something like, 'Stop this from happening to another thousand-year-old tree'?" Veronica asked. "With the website URL, of course. Then, 'Save Sky River Valley by donating to a craft guitar shop that will build instruments out of salvaged lumber, instead of clearcutting these ancient trees.' Or something like that."

Nathan typed into the computer. "That'll work. I just need to get this satellite internet feed hooked up." He flipped open the latches of a black briefcase, then started plugging wires into his laptop. "Okay, team. Live around the world in five."

"Clete, how about you help me take a larger piece off one of these Sitka spruces," Uncle Cliff said. "Like that one you found. I want a bigger chunk."

Clete leaped down from the cedar, landing in a crouch. "Do you want to run the saw? Or do you want me to?"

"Well, all right, big guy. You can run it, seeing as how you just cut down the king of the forest."

"I'm not proud of it."

"I know you're not."

Clete poured gas from one of the red containers, then bolted the chainsaw to the Alaskan mill. He pulled the cord, and the saw screeched to life. Cliff took the other side, and helped push the blade along the length of the tree. The engine screamed as the chain dug deeper, and a plume of dark wood lightened as the bar worked through. At the far end Cliff powered the saw down. "On three. One, two, three."

They heaved the moss-heavy skin, stepping back as it tumbled off the tree. The bright yellow wood beneath seemed to glow from within, casting a wan light over Clete's features. It reminded Nicky of the buttercups her mother used to hover beneath their chins, dappling their skin golden. "You girls both love butter."

Cliff rapped the wood with his knuckles, nodding. "Amazing. This wood is pristine. Just as you kids said."

Danny came over and ran a finger along the grain. "Cell structure's perfect. I would pay double for wood like this. The music this would make."

"It's just gorgeous wood," Uncle Cliff said. "You get the natural crowding in a grove like this, making the growth circles tight."

"Okay, Daniel," Nathan called from where he stood by the spruce. "You want to stand by with your axe? I've put up notices all over social media. Seattle and Silicon Valley are standing by. They'll seed it once we get going. Thirty seconds until we go out to the world."

Their father returned to where he had been standing. He lowered the brass slide over his pinkie. The body of the guitar rose and fell as he settled it against his chest. "I'm out of practice for performing," he said.

"Well, get ready," said Nathan, pushing his glasses up the bridge of his nose. "Who's introducing you?"

"Nicky, this was all your idea," Josie said, the admiration clear in her voice. "You do it."

Nicky shook her head. "No. You and Veronica. You're a good team."

Veronica stepped forward. She lifted the purple mask with the Alaska flag off her mouth and stood next to their father, almost matching his height. "Maybe you introduce?" she said to Josie. "Then I'll make the ask."

"I'll do it, girls," Alice said. "I'm the mayor, after all."

"Everything's linked up," Nathan said. "Folks are ready, let's not keep 'em. Alice, then Veronica, then Josie, and music. Josie, you do outro. Good?"

All of them nodded.

"Okay. I've sent out the link. Looks like we're starting with just over a thousand viewers. It's up to you to get more. On my mark. Counting down from ten, nine eight, seven, six, five, four . . ." He finished with his fingers, and pressed the button. Nicky inhaled as the red light came on and Alice started to speak.

CHAPTER THIRTY

"**G**ood morning, good afternoon, good evening," Alice started, delivering a genuine, welcoming smile that Nicky had never seen before. "We are coming to you via live satellite feed from the Tongass rainforest in Southeast Alaska. We are on Shee Island, just outside the town of Jackson Cove, population two thousand, where I happen to be mayor. No matter your time zone, we are glad to have you with us. We have a message for you from the youth of our small town. Meet Veronica Deschumel and Josephine Hall. These courageous middle schoolers have been pressing to save a valley of old-growth trees behind Jackson Cove, and you'll want to help them. Veronica?"

Veronica stepped into the frame, giving a friendly wave to the camera, then breaking into her winning smile. "Hello, friends. Today, less than a mile from where I stand, gas-powered saws are ready to cut down these trees you see all around me. It is a day of loss and pain, not just for this forest, but for our community, and for Earth. The tree I stand in front of, which was cut this morning, is over a thousand years old."

Nathan put two thumbs up, mouthing the words "Three thousand viewers and climbing!"

"We have a chance to stop this disaster," Veronica continued, taking another step forward, and gesturing with her hands to the forest around her. Nicky noticed that she wore the same wool turtleneck sweater as she had on the welcome video she had sent. "The mill that is supposed to cut these trees has the opportunity to convert to a craft guitar shop. Instead of killing these ancient trees, like this thousand-year-old yellow cedar behind me, we can use salvaged Sitka spruce to build instruments. This is Mr. Hall beside me, a guitar maker and my neighbor. He holds in his hands a guitar made from Sitka spruce."

Their father held up the guitar up by the neck, showing it to the camera. Nicky saw that the number of viewers had climbed to more than five thousand.

"Now I'd like to give you Josephine Hall, to introduce our musician."

Veronica stepped aside. Nicky looked at Josie, who turned back to her with a frightened expression. "I can't!" Josie said.

"What?"

"It was your idea. Go," she said, pushing Nicky. Nathan watched them, motioning for someone to step forward. Nicky's legs wouldn't budge.

"Nicky!" Josie said. "Please. I'm scared."

Nicky was too. Then she leaned over and touched the cap of a chanterelle. Instantly, she felt a buzzing. The trees—they were listening as well. The current filled her with hope, and courage.

Taking a deep breath, she stepped into the frame.

"Hello. This is Nicky Hall. I'm actually Josie's twin sister. I'm here for all the people in my community, asking you to help. Donating any amount to this project would allow the mill to retool to make guitars. By giving, you would preserve this living, breathing forest for generations to come." She paused, staring hard into the lens of Nathan's camera. Her mind went blank. She knew there was more to say, but nothing came to her. She opened her mouth, and just started talking.

"My twin sister and I grew up in a small farming town in Pennsylvania. In April, our mother, an emergency room doctor, died of Covid-19. Our father brought us to this island just over a week ago." She found Josie's eyes. Her sister wasn't blinking as she watched her. "And even though we are new to this town, we came because we have family here—Aunt Mallory, and my Uncle Cliff, who works at the mill, and my cousin Clete. Today, we ask that you become new Alaskans too. My father, our father, will play you some music that these trees allow him to make. His name is Daniel Hall. He's an amazing man who has guided us through these tough times, to this extraordinary forest, which now needs your help."

Nicky leaned over to hug her father, smelling the wet cedar as she did. "Thanks, Nick," he told her.

He touched the brass slide to the strings, sending a few notes into the air. "Nicky already shared that we've had a tough year, just like so many of you around the world. Time heals, but music makes that healing go quicker. I built this guitar out of wood from trees like the ones around me. I know we're making a big ask—a moonshot, really—to believe we'll retrain loggers into guitar makers. But here in Alaska, we take the moonshots. If you live in the Lower 48, or anywhere else in the world, you could help us. If you love music, help us. If you love Mother Nature, and care about the future of our children, and this earth, please help."

Above him, the raven cawed, as if impatient for the music to start.

When you hear me singin' this old lonesome song,
People, you know these hard times can last us so long.

As he sang, Nicky could feel the earth beneath her vibrate. She touched the mushroom again. This time her knees went wobbly, the ligaments behind them loosening. The notes rising from the guitar and the pulses of energy combing through the earth swept through her. All at once she heard the trees, moving and speaking as one. *Nicky . . .*

You know that people are driftin' from door to door,
Can't find no heaven, no matter where they go.

Nicky closed her eyes, trying not to let panic break her down. The music surged with the sound of the trees, the two strains resolving toward a unified vibration, producing a single melody. *Thank you.*

With great effort she lifted her hand from the mushroom, and her boots from the earth, and set a hand on her father's shoulder, then another on the cedar, which felt warm to her, despite the moist bark. The last of her father's notes echoed among the tree trunks.

"Please," Nicky said. "Please help save Sky River Valley."

"And we're out," Nathan said, making his palm into a fist. "Wow. Norway, Morocco, Rio de Janeiro, Toronto. Number kept climbing. Nearly a hundred thousand viewers. I've never seen a live feed go that viral. Everyone, it seems, has eyes on Alaska."

"What about the page?" Josie asked, coming toward him. "GoFundMe. Is anyone donating?"

"That will take longer," Nathan said, watching his screen. "Though we're at just over a thousand dollars. I'll put this on YouTube now. And we'll see. But I think the internet likes us—like, a lot."

Uncle Cliff smiled, lifted his mesh cap from his head, and flattened his black hair. "Unbelievable." His eyes searched for Nicky, and he winked at her. "Can I use your satellite phone, Nathan? I think it's time I check in with Lars."

CHAPTER THIRTY-ONE

C liff pressed numbers into the phone, then brought the receiver to his ear. "Lars. I'm out here in the grove. We just cut into one of the spruces. It's good wood." Uncle Cliff paused, his brow creasing. "I can tell them that. Yes. I understand."

He listened for another moment, then covered the mouthpiece. "He said people from Denmark and Kenya are calling him to order guitars. From all over the world. Also, he's getting his lawyers involved."

"What else?" Nathan asked, pausing as he packed his equipment.

Cliff listened. "I understand. I hear you." He paused, gazing around the forest, a slow smile spreading across his face. "Roger that. I'll tell them."

He hung up. Everyone watched him.

"So?" Josie said. "Uncle Cliff, what did he say?"

"He said his great-grandfather came over to the United States to cut wood, and that's what he does. Also . . . that he's backing out on the deal to cut the valley. He doesn't want anything else to do with it. He's selling the mill."

Silence fell among them as they took turns staring at one another. Except Josie, who couldn't take her eyes off Nicky.

"Does he have a buyer?" Nathan finally asked.

"Why?" Cliff said. "Are you interested?"

Nathan shook his head. "I couldn't afford what he's asking, I'm sure. But would you be interested in running it?"

Uncle Cliff looked over at their father. "What do you think, *maestro*?"

"What do *I* think?"

"Would you run the floor? Teach us how to build guitars?"

Nathan started to snap together his steel briefcase. "Now, if that were the case, I *would* be interested in investing in a local guitar company. And I know a few others who might as well."

"As do I," Alice said. "I bet people from all over town would help get this off the ground. We'd be shareholders. An island-owned worker's cooperative."

"I do believe this is going to make the Alaska state wire," Aunt Mall said as she scribbled in her notepad. "And probably Alaska history."

Nathan flipped up the collar of his waxed coat. "Good work out here. Let's get back into town, and figure out how to buy ourselves a mill."

As they crossed over the second muskeg, a cool evening breeze blew through the trees along the fringe. The moss was turning wine-red, while the alders and devil's club around the muskeg shifted to a yolky yellow.

Her father stopped in the trail and waited for Nicky. "Hey, kiddo. My head is still reeling. How are you doing?"

"Hi, Dad. Me too. But I'm good."

"You two girls, both of you—I can't believe it. You found the solution."

Nicky smiled up at him. "I was just listening to the trees," she said honestly.

"Did I ever tell you, your mother swore that, when you were a baby, you wouldn't stop talking to that red oak across from the church? You'd crawl through the grass and just hang out by the trunk, babbling away. She was convinced you were having an entire conversation with that old guy."

"No," Nicky said, genuinely surprised.

"She said you'd drop into another world. Now I think she might have been right."

Nicky smiled at this, pleased with the new memory.

"It's funny, because me, I was scared of the woods as a child. Grandpa told us that monsters lived in the woods around Danville. They had long nails and would scrape off your skin. I guess I've always been scared of trees, and the forest," he said, looking ahead at Mallory. "Maybe that's why I like taming them into guitars."

Aunt Mall walked in long strides in front of them. Cliff had an arm around her waist, and held her close. They passed where Nicky had seen the bear earlier that morning.

It felt like ages ago when she had stood right there, so sad and alone. And scared.

Nicky ran her fingers along the bark of a tree. An image of herself, or perhaps her own children running their small fingers along the bark, flashed before her. "I was thinking," Nicky said to her father, "that maybe, once the mill gets going, you might need an apprentice."

"Good idea!" he said. "Know anyone?"

"Clete?"

"I was thinking of all of you—Veronica, Clete, you, and Josie. At least, when Josie and Veronica don't have debate after school."

Nicky looked ahead, where Clete and Josie talked together, their twin buns bouncing as they made their way between the trees. The green in Josie's hair had started to fade, her strawberry blond pushing back through.

"That sounds so cool."

Word had gotten out that the Old Yellow Cedar had been cut, and a few of the loggers had come out to witness the behemoth lying on the ground. One of them now walked with Veronica and Nathan, the plastic mask of his orange helmet pulled over his face. Nicky recognized the handkerchief around his neck. It was the same worker who had brought her up to Uncle Cliff at the mill. Nathan smiled as the man gestured, explaining something about the woods.

The trail cut toward the river, and Josie drifted back to join them. The current grew louder, and she raised her voice as she spoke. "I actually think Watermelon would like it in these woods," Josie said. "Next summer when it's warm, we'll bring her out. What do you think?"

"Sure," Nicky said. "I think she'd love the moss. And the salmonberries."

"Imagine that. An Alaskan iguana. Clete knows the name of every plant. He even has the Latin memorized. He's an encyclopedia."

Nicky watched him up ahead, running his hands through a berry bush, eating a few. "I told you our cousin was cool."

The afternoon sun splintered through the needles. Nicky combed her fingers through a huckleberry bush, managing to capture a single red pea-sized berry. The arch of her foot settled onto a tree root, and a sensation of delight went up her boot.

"I've got a question for Nathan," their father said. "You girls talk. I'll be back."

They both watched as their father walked ahead. Then Josie stopped in the trail and took Nicky by the shoulder. She turned her sister so the two faced each other.

"Hey," Josie said, staring back at her. Then she leaned over and hugged Nicky. Even through her wet windbreaker, Nicky could feel the beat of Josie's heart. Her wet hair brushed Josie's cheek.

"Maybe you can teach me," Josie whispered into Nicky's ear. "You know, how to listen."

Nicky surveyed the forest over her sister's shoulder, then looked up into the layers of needles fanned out above her.

"Okay," Nicky said, trying to imagine what the trees

might say to her sister. "Maybe you can teach me to dye my hair."

Josie pulled back, her eyes going wide with surprise. "Really?"

"Sure," Nicky said. "Purple?"

"You would look *so cool*. I was going to do mine in pink next. Dad's gonna flip out."

"Dad will be fine," Nicky reassured her.

Josie nodded. "You're right. He'll be fine."

They started walking again. At the cedar bridge, Josie climbed the stump stairs, picking her way across. She stopped in the middle, and the two of them looked down into the water, watching their mottled reflections, drained of color.

"We could be the same person," Nicky said.

"No," Josie said, staring back at her through the water. Then she smiled. "Mine look so new compared to yours."

At first Nicky thought she was talking about their faces, and started to laugh. Then she saw how Josie lifted one of her boots and was examining it in the low forest light. "They still look so new."

"I thought you said you'd never wear them," Nicky said.

"People change, I guess," Josie said, staring at the toe of her boot. "Maybe I'll even wear them to school."

"I thought you were going back to Danville," Nicky said, gently elbowing her.

"Watermelon likes it here," Josie said after a moment, elbowing her back.

Nicky watched her sister skip the length of the cedar,

continuing along the trail on the opposite bank. Then she looked upstream, toward the back of the valley.

She bent her head to examine her wrists, the blue veins running up her arms, taking blood from her heart and swirling it back. To her heels, up through her legs, into her head. Completing a circuit that allowed her to stand here, on this bridge, noticing this island carved by glaciers from the sea. Upright in the pine-scented, briny air, rooted in the living dark beneath her.

She felt a pull, and looked down into the water. Her gaze dropped beneath the stones, into the soil, thick with veins connecting the trees. "Hi, Mom," Nicky said, staring along the length of the river. "I miss you, but you taught us so well."

She stood for a moment longer. The current flowed hard and true at her feet, emerging from the dark of the valley toward the open ocean.

Then she took a breath, crossed the bridge, and ran to catch up with her sister.

A NOTE TO THE READER

I want to thank you, the reader, for taking the leap of faith required to move through these pages alongside Nicky, Clete, Veronica, and Josie. I hope they have left you with a sense of urgency, but also a feeling of possibility, and perhaps even responsibility.

Now that you've read *Whispering Alaska*, I'd like to tell you a bit about how I came to call Alaska home. A breath, really. That's all it took. But here's the longer story.

At the age of nineteen, twenty-three years ago, eager to leave the city and find forest not interrupted by farms and towns, I boarded a Greyhound bus in Philadelphia. I traveled first to California, then up the coast to the Pacific Northwest, before boarding a plane to Alaska.

It was September, the days already shortening. We lifted off in the evening, Seattle's swirl of lights giving way to shapes of tree-covered mountains to the east, the new-fallen snow on the craggy tops reflecting the light of the moon. After a couple of hours, a single strip of light along the coast of an island appeared. We touched down in Sitka, where I stepped out of the airport, inhaling the briny, faintly astringent scent of rainforest and sea.

But I still wasn't close enough.

After a few months working at the salmon hatchery, I moved out of my log cabin apartment into the woods, about twenty minutes outside of town. Using gangion line, I strung a corridor of tarps and lived at the far end, in a butterscotch North Face VE-25 tent. I whittled a spoon from yellow cedar, pouring three packages of shrimp ramen into a blue enamel bowl, which I boiled over a fire. Fall storms such as the one at the end of *Whispering Alaska* blew down from the north, shredding my corridor of tarps. Cold set in. I'd arrive home at night to find my tent coated in hoarfrost. One evening, while trying to prime my camp stove inside the tent to build a bit of heat, I burned down my vestibule. Despite spending time on my uncle's farm as a kid—in Danville, as you might have guessed—I spent most of my childhood in the city. I had no idea what I was doing.

After a few months I packed up my sleeping bag and moved to another spot, on a hill by Kaasda Héen—Indian River. I cut down saplings and built a hut, filling the spaces between the branches with jars of olive oil and cans of soup. I lived there for the next five months.

Each evening after work I returned to my site, the cedar boards in the muskegs bending beneath my weight, burping up muddy water, the northern lights shivering above Gavan Ridge. I became good at drying wood and building fires, pulling my scarred pot from the hemlock embers with pliers. Afraid of attracting brown bear with the smell of mint, I stopped brushing my teeth at night, falling asleep with the spice of cedar in my mouth, surrounded by trees swollen with the flesh of salmon.

As winter wore on, I began reading about the history of my new home. I learned that the indigenous Tlingit had inhabited Sheet'-ká X'áat'l—or just Shee, meaning "The Island"—for ten thousand years, give or take, before the Russians settled in Old Sitka, in 1799. I read about how the Russians, eager to build ships large enough to stand up to the fleets of the Spanish, Germans, British, and upstart Americans, fashioned masts from the oldest trees, before selling Alaska to a young, war-torn United States. America took up where the Russians had left off, except now on an industrial scale, logging the valleys and coasts, before clearing the sides of mountains.

On walks back to my hut, I began to pick out great stumps, large as cars, crumbling back into the earth. I pictured men in wool vests swinging their broad, barbed axes, chanting Russian folk songs as spruce trees crashed to the ground. At night, crawling into my sleeping bag, I imagined that the trees all around my hill whispered stories of annihilation as bolts of energy trembled through the soil.

Spring fell over the island. One sunlit March afternoon, I hiked back into the fan of the valley. I crossed and recrossed rivers, finding a wide bear trail that cut through a muskeg dotted with dwarf pines, their branches hung with aquamarine strands of old man's beard. The spongy moss, bright with new growth, flexed beneath my boots. Holding my hands to my face, I pushed through a thicket of golden devil's club. The temperature plunged, while around me rose ancient behemoth trees with trunks as thick as lighthouses. I was standing in a grove of undisturbed old growth, with trees hundreds, if not thousands, of years old, just like Nicky and Clete.

Since that spring day, I have hiked from the house in Sitka where I now live with my family back to that stand of old growth, to hunt, or just to roam, any number of times. I have clambered up the slopes of the Three Sisters, mountains that rim the valley, and walked to the root of the valley, where a glacier-fed waterfall pours into a turquoise pool. I have fished for Dolly Varden trout, watching as alder leaves drop into the current, moving toward the ocean. I've watched salmon school up each year up at the mouth of the river, beginning a journey upstream to lay eggs at the point of their own hatching. And I have watched the brows of friends from the Lower 48 soften as they bear witness to all this, a hush of wonder moving over them.

When my oldest daughter was about eight months old, I took her to my first campsite along the muskeg, where I burned down the vestibule of my tent from all those years ago. It was late summer, and the few remaining pink salmon, chalky with age, finned against the current. Devil's club, just starting to turn yellow, grew over salmon carcasses, their eyes picked clean by eagles. Mushrooms shiny with moisture pushed up from the rich earth. As we stood there beneath the crowns of the hemlocks, she stared up at me with her big hazel eyes, her chest rising and falling.

Over the last few hundred years, salmon streams around the world have been filled in, paved over, just as the forests that feed these fish oxygen have been obliterated. Scotland, Norway, Connecticut—lands where salmon once thrived and trees grew tall—now have only patches of forest left, and a few token vestiges of salmon runs. The Greek word *krisis* means "turning point in a disease." We are at such a turning point now.

Covid-19, of course, is about breathing as well. As you've read, Josie and Nicky's mother dies from lack of breath, sending her children and husband on their own journey across the country, which ends in a seaside town similar to Sitka. Both Josie and Nicky realize, in their own ways, that attacking the earth—especially the forests—is akin to attacking ourselves. Logging, global warming, forest fires, ocean acidification—how many ways can our planet choke at once?

As you've read *Whispering Alaska*, I hope you have been able to breathe beside Nicky, Josie, Veronica, and Clete. I hope you could taste the citrus scent of spruce and hemlock needles, and that your own heart rushed as the brown bear rose from the devil's club, and that you could taste the spice of the Old Yellow Cedar on the back of your tongue. Maybe you'll even feel some of the same wonder staring up at the crowns of these great trees as Nicky does when she follows Clete into the forest, and as I did that spring. Alone in the forest, chest rising and falling, almost hearing the trees breathe, giving back pure oxygen. Allowing all of us together, across this planet, to breathe.

If you'd like to continue the work of the foursome in this book, you'll find on the following pages a number of environmental groups in Alaska to reach out to. I've also included a few suggestions for further reading—a list by no means exhaustive, but a starting point, for sure. Perhaps some of these writers will touch you with their commitment to understand how to live sustainably in one of the world's last wild lands, and their pure celebration on the page of what it means to be alive, and just breathe.

ALASKA ENVIRONMENTAL GROUPS
Alaska Rainforest Defenders
Alaska Wilderness League
Salmon State
Sitka Conservation Society
Southeast Alaska Conservation Council
Sustainable Southeast Partnership

SELECTED READING
Blonde Indian: An Alaska Native Memoir, Ernestine Hayes
The Dead Go to Seattle, Vivianne Faith Prescott
Fishcamp: Life on an Alaskan Shore, Nancy Lord
The Island Within, Richard Nelson
Ordinary Wolves, Seth Kantner
The Raven's Gift, Don Rearden
The Rising and the Rain: Collected Poems, John Straley
The Smell of Other People's Houses, Bonnie-Sue Hitchcock
The Stars, the Snow, the Fire: Twenty-Five Years in the Alaska Wilderness, John Haines
Unseen Companion, Denise Gosliner Orenstein
The Wake of the Unseen Object: Travels Through Alaska's Native Landscapes, Tom Kizzia
A Wolf Called Romeo, Nick Jans

ACKNOWLEDGMENTS

I owe a great debt of gratitude to those who tolerated my disappearances, in both body and spirit, over the course of the creation of this book. I hope these pages offer some small justification.

In particular, I'd like to thank Roby Littlefield, for help with the Tlingit language, along with her deep insight and knowledge into the bright and living Tlingit culture. Also to her son Ed Littlefield, for help in a clutch moment, and to Yéil Ya-Tseen, for bringing his calmness and thoughtfulness to difficult passages in the book. To S'áaxwshaan, for sharing myths found in these pages, and to Tammy Young and the Sitka Tribe of Alaska, for the consideration and helpfulness.

Un grand merci to Eléonore Bertrand for her encouragement, and for taking the time to share her deep knowledge of the phenomenon of twins. Also to Michaela Dunlap, who blends her deep knowledge of the Alaska rainforest with a generosity of spirit I've seldom encountered. A thank you in neon to the entire town of Sitka—I apologize to tourists and locals alike for playing fast and easy with geography, topography, cartography—really anything that might be graphed.

To the good folks at Sitka Conservation Society, whose

board I am proud to sit on: I am in awe of your tireless commitment not only to protecting old-growth forests, but also salmon streams, through commitment to programs like Fish to Schools, 4-H, and other strategies that help us live in the woods. Also to Andrew Thoms, whose dual commitment to community and the wild largely inspired this book. To Larry Edwards and the Alaska Rainforest Defenders, for constant vigilance; and to Nels, whose memory and artistic shadow in Alaska I'm proud to work beneath. Brent Cole at Alaska Specialty Woods inspired a critical part of this book and was incredibly generous with his time on the phone and over email.

Sara Anderson, Carrie Johnson, Katherine Kelton (a twin!), and Emma Libonati: thank you for helping me title this book. To Steve Gavin, a buddy always up for a careful, considered read: still waiting for you to come home. To Justin Ehrenwerth, sometimes it does hurt to be alive, brother. I'm only glad you're here to share this spin around the planet with me. To my boys Rick Petersen and Alexander Allison, for their observations no one outside Alaska could provide. And also to Mr. Allison's fire seventh-grade Language Arts class—your early corrections regarding both subsistence and the comportment of teenagers these days were clutch. To Marian Allen: your commitment to the Tongass is unmatched. To John Maxey, who provided shelter in Seattle so I could finish revisions, and Rob Sachs, whose reads and humor carried me through much of this. To Alex, for virtual beers during the pandemic, and Jeff Marrazzo, who provided a much-needed New Year's break, allowing me to focus on this book. A better friend one could not hope for.

To Rick Powers, whose tightly knotted slips of survey tape wave from the branches, blazing a trail all but impossible to follow—and yet still I try, proud of every step I land in your outsized tracks. To Dr. BJ Smith, whose medical advice—from a Pennsylvania doctor, no less—was indispensable. Thank you to Rachel Smith for her acute attention to the word even in a tough moment. To Suzanne Rindell, always the one in the open doorway—always—my companion along this rocky, fraught path.

To my editor, Beverly Horowitz, who hung tough through early versions—there's no one I'd rather receive an email from on a Sunday. To her assistant, Rebecca Gudelis, for her patience and thoroughness in the book's final stages. To Julia Masnick, my "baller" agent at Watkins/Loomis, whose wit is matched only by her thoughtfulness and professionalism. And to Gloria Loomis: thank you for the unerring guidance.

To Marina Pelmeneva, who forced me to describe this book in Russian, thus condensing the plot considerably. To Cora Dow, whose clarity as a powerful young Alaska forest activist helped create Josie's character, and to her mother, Rebecca Poulson, for her gorgeous illustrations. And to Sylvia Bi for the beautiful jacket and interior design, and to Rowan Kingsbury for the inspired jacket art.

To Aunt Mary Jo and Uncle Fred, whose warmth and generosity have saved me from darkness more than I'd ever like to acknowledge. To Denise Gosliner Orenstein, hippest aunt ever, and quickest reader. To my mother, Kathy Gosliner, for her constant love and presence, and unswerving faith in the word. To my stepfather, Joseph Lurie, for his considered reads, and for being a model on how to serve on this earth.

To Len Kola, for helping to watch the kiddos, and to my mother-in-law, Donna Lee, for the same—and for threatening to "go Sicilian" on anyone in the business who wrongs me. To my girls, for climbing over my legs and slapping the laptop closed, announcing that it's time to go outside to pick mushrooms or catch a fish. Also to Unicorn Kitty, who—though I hate her with everything inside me, down to her little rainbow horn—made the perfect pillow for my head. I couldn't have revised in the Airstream RV without her.

Finally, to the good grammar teachers in the Catholic schools my wife attended, who provided her with the tools to help me—when she's not dispensing justice on our small island in Alaska—wrangle ideas into a book. Rachel Jones is about the grittiest, most beautiful and astonishing human I've ever come across. It is my great good fortune to walk this life alongside her, and I can only give thanks to the great, unseen powers beneath and above us who made it so.

ABOUT THE AUTHOR

BRENDAN JONES lives in Alaska and works in commercial fishing. A Stegner Fellow at Stanford University, he received his BA and MA from Oxford University, where he boxed for the Blues team. His work has appeared in the *New York Times*, the *Washington Post*, the *Smithsonian*, the *Guardian*, *National Fisherman*, the *Philadelphia Inquirer*, *Ploughshares*, *Narrative Magazine*, the *Seattle Times*, *Sierra Magazine*, *Patagonia*, *Popular Woodworking*, and the *Huffington Post*, and on NPR. His debut novel, *The Alaskan Laundry*, won the Alaskana Award and was longlisted for the Center for Fiction First Novel Prize. He recently finished work on a Fulbright grant in Siberia, where he lived with his wife, two daughters, and dog.

@BrendanIJones